# THE
# DEAD
# OF
# WINTER

# THE
# DEAD
# OF
# WINTER

## A.B. Gibson

Merry Xmas!
Dan Gibson

| Library of Congress Control Number: | | 2015917010 |
|---|---|---|
| ISBN: | Hardcover | 978-1-5144-1565-8 |
| | Softcover | 978-1-5144-1564-1 |
| | eBook | 978-1-5144-1563-4 |

Print information available on the last page.

Rev. date: 10/14/2015

**To order additional copies of this book, contact:**
Xlibris
1-888-795-4274
www.Xlibris.com
Orders@Xlibris.com
720673

To my patient and understanding partner of twenty-three years, Scott Beard, who probably could have written this book himself in half the time. And to my mother, Barbara Gibson, who once aspired to be an author and to whom I owe my passion for crossword puzzles, intelligent conversation and repartee.

# Acknowledgments

My head had always been full of plots and characters, and long before I wrote *The Dead of Winter,* a goal of mine was to put some of those ideas to paper and write a book of popular fiction. How hard could it possibly be? Well, it turned out to be easy, except for the writing, editing and publishing parts. Thank you Scott Beard for supporting my crazy dreams and for helping me get over yet another finish line.

I would like to express my very great appreciation to Sarah Cowperthwaite, who was there at the beginning, and to Josh Mukai, who helped give so much shape to the screenplay. To Seth Ward for helping to fill in some empty spaces, and to Kim McDonald for help with graphics and image rendering.

To Sean Daniel Giampietro for his wonderful sketches and for partnering with me on *Pumpkin Menace.* Thank you to my sounding board Gay Jervey, who writes so well and shares my appreciation of the genre. To Steve O'Toole Photography for the head shot.

Thanks to Olympic Gold Medalist Dr. Tenley Albright, who encouraged me to include her signature beige figure skates as a weapon.

A special thank you to all the past employees and customers of Ridgefield Farm and Orchard, who unwittingly became the inspiration for this book.

# 1

*Still following.* She knows because when she stopped to check a moment or two ago, she could still hear him chasing her. She is hardly making any noise as she races through the cut paths of the maze, but her predator is barreling right through the corn, and his heavy boots are making a loud crunching sound. The turbulent noise from his arms and body crashing against the dry, brittle cornstalks is terrifying. And it is becoming louder.

The woman has rushed into the maze too quickly to even notice what direction she is going. She is paying more attention to the gash in her ribs than anything else, and she doesn't care about finding their so-called *exit* anyway. She only wants one thing—*out.* At first, the icy turns made it hard to go fast, and the sun, which was just beginning to rise, barely illuminated the paths. The first frost came early, and there have already been a few more since. She can't slow down, and she cannot fall.

A treetop stares over the field straight ahead, and the choices that quickly draw near are only to go left or right. Without breaking stride, she goes with her instinct and turns left, thinking if she keeps going in different directions, maybe she can lose him. Her legs wobble from speed and exhaustion, and she chokes on the biting wind that stirs the cornstalks.

By now she has lost a lot of blood from her deep wound, and she's feeling fainter than before, so she knows she must dig in mentally and keep running at full speed. Another choice to make. It's a left for the tall tree at the edge, which maybe she can climb up to see a way out, or a right to keep moving farther away from her assailant. She cuts this turn a little tight, and her feet fail to find solid ground under the frosted corn stubble. She slips, and the inertia of her full force slams her down face-first. Black silence for a few moments—nothing to see and nothing to hear.

Her head is too heavy to lift now, and now her heart is pounding, not from running but from fear. She opens her eyes, but her vision is blurry and bloodied, and she can only tell there is something dark under her face. The first swift kick knocks a few teeth out. Blood sprays out with her cry of pain. She's collapsed on her side, and the boot is above her face. She wants to scream, but the force comes down hard on her mouth before she can. She can't see at all and can barely hear. Instead she can only feel the rise and fall of whatever is smashing her head. She goes numb quickly, and then it's over. The blackness envelops her perception, and her mind shuts down. She experiences no more.

# 2

"**C**an we play on the pirate ship again, Mom?" asks the overactive seven-year-old. She's hopping up and down, hoping her best "Can I, can I?" smile will win over her not-very-gullible mother, who is watching her credit card being swiped on the iPad at the checkout counter in the little country store. "No, sorry, Brianna. We're going to Grandma's for dinner, remember?"

Today is the second to the last day of PumpkinFest, and Winter's Farm and Orchard is jammed with eager visitors and anxious parents scrambling to get their family pumpkins before Halloween. The shelves look a little empty today, just the way Ma and Pa like, thanks to customers like them and dozens of other panicky folks who have rushed to the farm, desperate to redeem their soon-to-expire social media coupons. The line to the cashier is always longest at the end of the day, and right now it begins all the way outside at the produce stands.

By design, customers are directed in a circuitous loop past every section of the little store to maximize opportunities for impulse buying, and those in line lug shopping baskets overflowing with jars of thick preserves and spicy apple butter. Books for sale arm urban visitors with fresh resolve not to just carve their pumpkins but to make a pumpkin pie from scratch. And not just to bake one pie but to bake more in general. Or try canning. *Maybe this will be the year to make pickles?*

Fall, of course, is their high season, showcased with crisper air, spectacular colors, and an abundance of fresh fruits and vegetables, many of which customers can pick for themselves. Customers flock to the farm for the main attractions, like the hayrides, the corn maze, the orchard, and the pumpkin patch, but they linger for the more passive and intrinsic joys of simply strolling through the beautiful property. For each visitor, Winter's Farm and Orchard is a custom fit and, in that sense, a little magical. Adults can reexperience nostalgic childhood outings by bringing their own kids to pick apples, flowers, and pumpkins. At Christmas, many return to brave the elements to cut down the family tree. For kids there is nonstop entertainment, junk food, and sensory overload. As the brochure for the farm states, "Winter's Farm and Orchard is your farm experience for every season."

But nostalgia is intangible and is impossible to bequeath, and every year there are parents who fail to convert a trip to the farm into a cherished new tradition. "Can't we just buy one already picked?" their kids would moan. For many of them, one insect is way too many, and it doesn't matter if it is too cold or too hot; it is just too much outdoors. Ma and Pa couldn't care less. Everyone paid, whether they had fun or not.

Across the main area in front of the busy store and a bit of a walk toward the southwest are the acres and acres of endless straight long rows of pumpkins known as the Pumpkin Patch. Closing time is soon approaching, and there are still plenty of families pulling small wagons, desperately searching for the "perfect" pumpkin. Ma and Pa know there is little they can do to get them to hurry along, because people never seem to know what they are looking for until they stumble upon it. The perfect pumpkin has to have a certain unspecified hue of orange or be perfectly cylindrical—or not! Maybe there should be a long stem, or maybe none at all. Some folks just won't be satisfied until they have inspected every single pumpkin in the ten-acre field. But the Winters have large wooden apple bins full of pumpkins in front of their store too for those who are in a hurry and for those customers who understand they are, after all, just buying pumpkins.

Just down from the little store, the hay wagon empties its passengers for its gazillionth and final time. The four wooden steps at the end of the wagon are pretty high off the ground, and the last step often requires assistance from Pa. Still, it is nearly impossible to keep kids from pushing each other off, and he often looks the other way to accommodate a little horseplay.

"Mom says this was my fifth hayride," one little eight-year-old girl proudly announces to her group.

"Well, this is my six thousandth millionth time," her friend counters confidently.

There is another line to take souvenir photographs at the Harvest Memories area in front of the store. One of the cutouts has been painted to look like a large pile of bright-orange pyramid of pumpkins, and people place their faces in the holes where some of the pumpkins have been cut out. The sign below it reads, "We picked our pumpkins at Winter's Farm and Orchard." There is always lots of pushing and shoving and jockeying into position at that cutout, because apparently some of the positions on the pile are more coveted than others, though neither Ma nor Pa can understand why.

But even as the Pumpkin Patch and the other activities around the farm are winding down, the Scary Giant Corn Maze is a different story at the end of the day. The maze of windy paths covers about ten acres, and there are always folks in there right up until closing. Some are lost, and some simply have misjudged how long it will take to go through. Most stay as long as they can, however, because it is so much fun.

Ma makes sure her boys get a head start getting every visitor off the property by five o'clock, because tonight there is another event catering to an entirely different crowd. In a little while, she will send in some of the younger boys to round up the stragglers and lost souls. They'll guide them out into the custody of impatient parents, who now, because of their lateness, will have to join the long backup of cars that snakes along at a crawl from the parking lot to the exit. She'll send in Lucas to root out the "party folks," who are named after the flotsam and jetsam they inevitably leave behind.

As folks leave, the exhausted crew begins to shutter the little concession stands and put away the remaining produce from the colorful wooden stands in front of the store. All of it is kept cool behind the massive sliding door of the huge walk-in next to the store. By six o'clock every day, the staff is tired of smiling and being hospitable, and by tomorrow at this same time after six weeks of PumpkinFest, everyone will really be ready to wrap it all up for the year. *Only one more day!*

By Monday at this time, the farm will resemble a normal residence, and the only thing left to remind them of the tourists will be a few large boxes of random sunglasses, toys, stray articles of clothing, and a couple of cameras. On that day the phone will be ringing all day, with anxious people eager to learn if their precious lost items have been found. They never are found, though, because on that same Monday, the Winters hold one of their very own family traditions—drawing straws for the lost treasures.

Ma stands in her place of honor at the edge of a landscaped circular area in front of the store, where she can say good-bye to each of the customers as they head to their cars. She looks up to the sky and notices darker clouds gathering in a portent of the promised storm later in the night, but she hopes her weatherman is right and they'll have time to hold the evening festivities before the bad weather comes.

"Well, Ma. You did it again! We had a blast as always," shouts one grateful single dad.

"Thanks for opening up your farm again," adds another, shaking her hand.

"Can you believe Tiffany is starting middle school?"

Ma responds with her signature "Lands sakes alive!"

"We'll be back at Christmastime for our tree," shouts a guy about to cram five kids into his bright-red monster truck. The youngsters will have to compete with firearms for space in the back.

"Don't forget it's the last night of haunting season tonight. We've got our traditional bonfire and that special hayride again!" Ma advertises to everyone she sees. "Starts when it gets dark."

# 3

**D**riving along, Josh stares deep into the darkening woods. He made an unfortunate wrong turn at a crucial point early on, and having had to backtrack over hours of winding roads has turned his mood sour. Back when his phone was pulling in two whole bars, he received a text from Dillon that he and Tara were just leaving, but that was several hours ago, and since then he's lost both satellite and GPS reception. *How can there not be any signal for fuck's sake?* He probably wouldn't have noticed, except his wife has been sleeping most of the trip, and he has had to drive in silence.

As he looks over to check his phone's signal again, he accidentally veers into the center of the narrow road. Just then, two headlights of an angry truck charge down at him from over the top of the steep incline on the narrow road, and he jerks the wheel hard to the right. It is a little too hard, and when their car runs over the huge ruts in the shoulder, his wife screams herself awake in the passenger seat.

"Josh! Your driving is freaking me out." Josh drifts back into his lane and speeds up as the road straightens a bit between empty fields.

"Sorry, but I was trying to use my phone to see where the hell we are," he partially lies. Julia and Josh, both in their thirties, have been married for six years, and their lack of communication shows the rust their relationship has begun to accumulate. She looks at him and then turns to the window and lowers it a bit.

Refusing to be ignored, Josh gets a little pissy. "I could have used your help, you know." Julia continues to stare out the window, comforted by the outside air. "Would you please at least talk to me?" Julia still refuses to acknowledge him, and his patience begins to wear. "You know I hate it when you do this." Her responses these days have boiled down to the irreducible minimum of what she needs to say, and countless fights have cut out much of the compassion he used to have for his wife. He glances her way again, tired of not being answered. "Damn it, Jules. Say something."

"Watch out!" she yells. The brakes squeal as Josh mashes the pedal to the floorboard. Their new car hops and skids closer and closer to a small child playing at the train crossing, and it squeals to a stop. They lower their windows.

"Jesus Christ, would you please pay attention to the road?" barks Julia, annoyed by any error he makes.

"Well, what the hell is he doing out here?" Josh says, pissed. "He should be home doing homework or something."

This fight has torn Josh's attention away from the road, and now their headlights expose a kid in raggedy clothes wearing a hood that seems to be made out of burlap and painted like a scarecrow face. The child barely seems to notice them, and it's not clear if he would have moved out of the way had they not stopped. He opens the door and stands up to speak to the boy, but the child scampers off into the coverage of the surrounding woods, and Josh loses sight of him.

"Hey!" he yells after him without moving far from the car. Julia emerges too, and they survey their surroundings. It's cold, and all the trees are beginning to look thin. They all bend and shiver in the wind. Josh shouts at the departed kid again, "Go home! It's dangerous out here, and it's getting late!" No response from among the trees until the wind picks up and stirs a low commotion. Is that what they hear, or is that the boy laughing at them? They can't be certain. Still shaken from the sudden surprise, the couple gets back in their car to escape the cold air. "Are you okay?" Josh asks Julia.

"I'm fine," she says dryly.

Josh is visibly annoyed but says nothing. He just keeps driving further and deeper on a road that's growing bumpier and windier. Eventually it slows them to a crawl. *Good thing*, he thinks to himself, because now he has to worry about running over kids playing in the middle of a road that was already too narrow for cars in both lanes. He decides to try holding a small conversation with Julia again: "Where the hell are we?" Julia squints at the road ahead and then suddenly reaches for Josh's forearm. He's taken by surprise by the act of affection.

"Stop!" she commands. Josh slams on the brakes again, and Julia strains to read a cracked wooden sign off to the side.

"We're here."

"Winter's Farm and Orchard," she finally deciphers aloud, squinting through the dark. "Yeah, this is it. Pull in."

# 4

The road to the old farmhouse is long, apparently too long for them to pave, and despite the technology of their brand-new Mercedes, they and the car bump along violently, fully experiencing each pothole that pockmarks the sparse gravel of its surface. By now it's dark and Josh can scarcely see, but still he does a pretty good job weaving around them by channeling his downhill slalom skills. What the headlights do reveal are dozens of scarecrow-like figures with pumpkins for heads appearing to stand guard on either side of the winding driveway.

Josh slows the car to a crawl to get a better look. There's a doctor in a white coat with a stethoscope examining a patient, and a fetching starlet with very blond hair and huge boobs exploding from her sequined gown. A fireman, a lumberjack, and a schoolmarm are all dressed and posed to fit their occupations. For a moment, Julia forgets she's feeling petulant and becomes a little engaged. She squints and strains her eyes to appreciate the details. "Is that one holding a Coach bag?" she asks incredulously. "It can't be!" To Josh, the cut of the blazer on one dashing pumpkin gentleman looks like it might have been Armani.

"Hey, this place has some style," he cracks, speeding up when they spy what looks like the house a little farther up ahead. Momentary happiness is fleeting for Julia, and after they pass the last of the scarecrows, she slumps back down in her seat and remembers she's in a bad mood.

# 5

"**W**hat about the wine?" Tara asks, waving around a half-full glass. Dillon's glass is empty already. Tara looks at her glass. "Chug, chug, chug," Dillon taunts.

The two have been wandering around the farm for the last couple of hours, waiting for the rest of their group to assemble, when bouncing headlights announce the arrival of Josh and Julia. "I wonder if they had trouble finding this little hideaway," Tara wonders aloud as she watches her friends pull up to the quaint old farmhouse. "Or did they just leave late and not allow enough time as usual?" A little of the wine she was drinking has sloshed onto her shirt, leaving a telltale stain.

"Jeez, their car is like a spaceship—it can practically drive itself—and Josh is always so completely wired. I can't believe they could have gotten lost," Dillon mutters.

Tara's mind snaps back to the present. She drains the glass in two swigs and hands Dillon her wineglass. "I wish I had bought one of these bags when we were in Ouarzazate," Dillon confesses, as he unzips the handmade woven bag she has slung over her shoulder. "I always regretted it."

"I know, and remember the deal I negotiated for two of them? I take mine everywhere. It's one of those miracles, you know? It's real light, but it can hold an astonishing amount of stuff."

"Like today's contraband. How else would we have been able to sneak around with this wine?"

"I know, but who could last three days with Josh and Julia without a little buzz? I hope they're not going to be at each other's throats." Dillon mimes putting a gun to his head. Tara laughs, and he pulls the pretend trigger. They both have learned that if there's trouble with anything, Josh and Julia will transform it into trouble for everyone.

"Does it really say *no drinking* here?"

"Yeah, didn't you see the sign?" Tara smirks. "Josh will be pissed."

"I didn't see anything on the website about no drinking."

"Website, what website?"

"Yeah, come to think of it, I guess I just assumed they had one. Weird. What business doesn't have a website?"

"Now that I've seen the place, it's really not so weird."

"So how many bottles do we have?" Dillon rummages through her bag, making space for their glasses and the empty bottle.

"I only brought wine for the two of us," she replied. "I hope they had the sense to bring their own."

"Oh well, we can always go explore one of the small burgs around here and pick up some more." He zips up the bag.

"Yeah. I'm sure there's a great selection of wine out here," he says sarcastically. "Stuff made out of peaches or elderberry or something."

Tara and Dillon seem to be the perfect couple. They've been close friends since being set up on a blind date years ago by some of their circle of friends. They've become great companions, from both the short trips they took together, like this one out to the country, and from some longer wild and crazy travel adventures in Thailand and India. It helps that they are both fitness fanatics; Tara set records in every school she attended and is always training for some marathon or another. Dillon, however, never trained at anything; he is just a perpetual natural at every sport. And they both like their wine. But their mutual dry sense of humor and their shared curiosities about people and the world strengthens their bond. Neither threatened the other; they found that out right away on that first blind date, when Dillon set things straight, right off the bat, by telling her he was gay. She was pissed at first--but at their friends, not at him. They weren't the only ones to know, he insisted. It had been complicated.

"Come on," Dillon leads. "Let's go see what took them so long."

# 6

Josh and Julia pull up in front of the large white hundred-and fifty-year-old house that would host them tonight, and they pop open the trunk. Muffled conversation between them crescendos in volume as Josh steps around to yank out their matched luggage and set them on the lawn alongside their car. He feels under fire from Julia as he rummages around, looking for something she obviously felt was critical to their trip. "Are you kidding me? I asked you twice if you packed it. Twice. Do I have to do everything myself?" He slams the trunk shut.

"Howdy, folks." So he doesn't have to respond to Julia, Josh turns his attention to the innkeepers, who have stepped forward to greet them. "Welcome to Winter's Farm and Orchard Farm and Orchard. I'm Ma."

"And I'm Pa."

"We're the Winters!" they add in practiced unison.

"Howdy, we're the Peeles," Josh replies without even thinking.

Wrenches and screwdrivers jingle from his grease-stained leather tool belt, when Pa steps forward to shake Josh's hand. "Sorry if I stink. Been working on a motor," he adds with a simple nod to Julia.

"Pa's always tinkering around fixin' sumthin' for me," Ma says, beaming proud as can be.

They both appear to be somewhere in their sixties, but farm life has taken its toll, and it's likely they are actually much younger. Josh thinks Pa lives up to the stereotype of what men are supposed to look like in these parts, complete with his scent: a peculiar concentration of tobacco with intriguing nuances of grease and oil. Ma is a handsome, sturdy woman, and she radiates kindness. She's a caretaker; she knows her home and guests better than anyone. Julia hopes she will remember to tell her friends she thought Ma smelled like apples.

Ma looks from Josh to Julia, sensing the tension that she has just disrupted, but she smiles all the same. "Why, y'all are jest about the purtiest folks I ever did see, ain't they, Pa?" Ma's Appalachian accent is thick.

Julia recalls no other occasion when Josh used the word *howdy*, and she reprimands him. "Don't patronize them, Josh."

"I'm not patronizing anyone." Josh zips the bags closed again. "Come on. We'll find those things later."

"You're unbelievable." She glares at him, half-ignoring the hosts.

"I'm sorry if I can't keep track of everything."

"You weren't in charge of keeping track of everything. You were only in charge of a few things." Josh snatches the bags.

"Please, let us help you," Ma offers. She turns to the house. "Lucas! Lucy!"

A young man and a woman in their midtwenties dutifully hustle down to the car at the sound of Ma's voice. Lucy's long, stringy brown hair hangs lifeless and frames a face of unremarkable features, and on top of her head, she wears an anachronistic bonnet. The effect of projecting a little homespun authenticity is diminished by her bright-red tube top. Lucas is slightly taller than the large-boned Lucy, and his features and style are more refined. He wears designer jeans and a goofy straw hat that matches Pa's. Julia looks back and forth between Ma, Pa, and the two kids in search of some family resemblance, but she doesn't immediately find any and chalks it off to just being too dark to be able to tell.

"Kindly help our good-looking new guests with their belongings, dears." As Lucas moves to see to their bags, the front door flings open, and out bound seven or eight children, about half of whom are wearing the same burlap head covering they saw the boy on the railroad tracks wearing earlier. They chase and wrestle and run around the yard until Ma barks, "All right now, y'all! Cain't you see we have guests? Stop that ballyhoo, remember yer manners an' come up and introduce yerselfs."

Clearly Ma's commands carry a lot of weight, for they immediately form a single-file line, and the boys extend a hand to shake, and the girls each curtsy. The genders of the masked ones remain a mystery, as none of the kids speaks a single word. The spot where Josh and Julia were standing is geographically only a couple hours away from their home in the nation's capital, but at seven thirty that Friday evening, their intriguing new surroundings seem a million miles away. Julia would kid to her friends later that night that Josh must have taken a wrong turn through some sort of space and time portal, while she was asleep in the car.

The kids all wear a hodgepodge of clothing and mismatched outfits, but Julia thinks one of the girls might be wearing a Donna Karan sweater from last season. *Can't be—too out of place—and who would roll around on the ground wearing Donna Karan?* But again it is dark, and it is hard to be sure.

"Welcome to our farm." When Lucy extends her arms out wide and gives Josh a big bear hug, he is taken by surprise, but he's not offended, and he smiles and returns the hug with a few light taps on her back with his hand. She presses against him a little too hard and hugs a little too long, though, and the incident becomes awkward for everyone. Fortunately, it's interrupted by voices coming from behind them.

"It's about damn time!" Tara teases as she and Dillon materialize from the darkness.

"Let's put 'em in Suite Number 7." Ma waves her hand as though to give the order, and Lucy grabs the smallest. Lucas picks up the other three.

"You didn't say we were getting a suite, Josh." The unexpected upgrade makes a pronounced change in her attitude, and suddenly the place and her hosts seems more charming.

"Well, looky here." Ma eyeballs Dillon and Josh, who are now standing next together. "Y'all might be the best purtiest couple a men we ever did have on the farm, whaddya think, Pa?" He grunts, and Dillon and Josh blush a little at being called *purty* again.

"Why, thank you, ma'am, and you have a beautiful farm here. We've enjoyed exploring it a little, and we are looking forward to seeing the rest." He and Tara turn to their friends in the dark. "We were afraid it might end up just being the two of us here."

Josh offers a cautious little laugh. "No such luck, you're stuck with us tonight." Tara and Dillon share a quizzical look. "Tonight? What do you mean, tonight? You're not staying the whole time? Why didn't you tell us?"

Julia answers for both of them but avoids looking Tara and Dillon in their faces. "We're leaving a little early—Sunday morning now, as it turns out—because I need to spend some time with my mom."

"That's barely enough time to catch up!" Tara whines, but she's still hopeful. "Come on! You are gonna love this place. We got here a little while ago just as people were leaving, and you should have seen all the cars. This place was hopping, and tomorrow's going to be a blast."

Julia folds her arms in front of her out of a recent habit. "I know, Tara, but it's really important. I just don't think we can stay until Monday."

"Jeez, one of the biggest corn mazes in the state is sitting right here, and they've got an apple orchard where they let you pick your own apples. And"—turning to Ma Winter—"tomorrow you still have another day of your big festival, don't you, Ma?"

"Oh, ain't you sweet, you precious thing. Why yes, tomorrow is the last day of our annual Pumpkin Festival. Should be a mighty fine end to it too. God willing we'll have a right nice crowd. We got hayrides, a pumpkin patch, an' apples on the trees. A good harvest festival gets everyone ready for winter around here, and after tomorrow—well, we all hunker down for a long winter's rest."

Tara looks to Julia again. "Jules, did you hear that? Stay here that extra night, please. I hardly ever see you anymore, and Dillon and I made a special trip to see you two."

Julia sighs and adds, "It's been a while since I've seen her."

"It's been all of two weeks." Josh catches a frosty look from his wife. "What? C'mon!" Tara retorts. "Ma, tell her you want them to stay."

Ma shoots Pa a side look and then asks the children, "What do ya think, kids?"

"Stay! Stay!" they respond in unison, dancing for added emphasis.

"Pa?"

"Well, Ma, I can tell ya like 'em, so I think we should keep 'em as long as we can."

Tara intervenes, "See, Tara? Everyone wants you to stay. Please."

"We'll see. Okay? Best I can do."

Tara and Dillon show their disappointment, but it's the nervous looks from Ma and Pa that register the true panic of this sudden turn of events. "Hmm. Well, an' we had y'all down fer three nights." She hesitates, fishing for a response from Josh.

"Yeah, sorry." He pauses, clueless at first, then "Oh, that. Yes. Of course we'll pay you for the whole time."

Ma is relieved. "Since y'all aren't planning to be here as long as we figured, we'll just have to get the fun started right away, now won't we? Would y'all fancy a little cider?"

Josh is the quickest to respond again, "I'll fancy anything to turn up."

"Oh, this here's got a kick, dearie." Ma winks.

"What about the 'No Alcohol' sign we saw?" Dillon asks.

"Oh, that ol' sign's not fer y'all. It's for thems that stop by the festival during the day. We always like our house guests to feel free and feel at home."

"And all this time we've been sneaking around with a wine bottle in Tara's bag. I'm feeling more at home already."

"Okeydoke then. We're about to start up a big ol' bonfire down yonder if y'all want to head over and get comfy." Ma gestures toward a grassy pasture in the distance where a flame suddenly roars up. "We'll bring the cider down there for y'all, the good stuff," she adds with a devilish smile.

"Young man, I'll park your car fer ya. I need to park it in a special place 'round back, so it's not in the way of the crowd tomorrow," Pa adds before everyone leaves. "Got the keys?"

"They're still in the car, I think, Pa."

Dillon moves between him and Julia and puts his arms around their shoulders. Tara joins them, yelling, "Group selfie!"

"As one of the official purtiest guys at the farm, I'd just like to say it's a pleasure to hang with the two purtiest gals! What are the odds? Let's get the party started." Josh is happy to be around his old friends again, and he thinks the weekend can be salvaged after all.

# 7

Julia makes a move for the house, but Tara intercepts her. "Where do you think you're going?"

"Oh, Tara, I need to clean up a bit and maybe change my clothes. I wasn't planning to go straight to a bonfire, and I'm not really dressed for . . ."

"Sorry, Jules, but under the circumstances, you are no longer in charge. I am, and we're going straight to the bonfire. You've kept us waiting long enough. Now let's go!"

Dillon takes the lead, and the others follow him in the dark in the direction of the fire. They pass alongside the side and back of the house, which looks quite different from the front. The front retains the quaint charm of its one hundred-and-fifty-year-old architecture, but it's deceiving, because the rest of the house just rambles on and on, its original architectural integrity debased by one addition after another.

"I hope they let us explore the house," Tara mentions in passing. "It looks fascinating. You and Josh should find a big place like this. I can see the whole *Green Acres* thing happening but with lots of kids running around."

"Very funny, Tara."

Here and there primitive little hand-painted directional signs on wooden posts point to various farm attractions like Rollicking Hayride, Confusing Corn Maze, and Pumpkin Patch. The "Bonfire That-a-Way" sign is superfluous tonight, though, as its flames are tall and sparks are flying. The group can already hear its snap, crackle, and pop. Other guests already are laughing and chatting around the fire on blankets and tree stump stools.

"I can't wait to taste the cider. Shelly told me that it's amazing." Tara is sharing a blanket with Dillon.

"Oh my god, Shelly! I completely forgot about her. Where the hell is she anyway? Did she bail on us?" Josh asks. He's sitting beside Julia, who has barely made eye contact with anyone. He thinks she seems happy just to be staring at the fire. Sorting shit out, he hopes.

"It was totally last minute, Josh." Tara pauses. "It was totally last minute. Josh," she repeats louder this time. It was typical of Josh to ask a question and not listen for the answer. He finally looks over but not quite all the way. "She didn't bail. She was having trouble finding a sitter, but I thought she was going to try to come out yesterday. You'd know, Josh, if you read your texts and e-mail from your friends once in a while."

The conversation drops silent for a moment, and when Julia turns her head right to follow the noisy arrival of Ma and Lucy, everyone follows her gaze, eager for something a little upbeat.

"Here we are—a whole jug, and our good glasses," she announces proudly. She is carrying a serving tray with four tall glasses, all souvenirs from D-List tourist attractions. Lucy scampers into view right behind her, cradling a heavy ceramic jug straight out of an old *Li'l Abner* cartoon strip. It is all they could hope for—brown with a white stripe and a fat cork on top.

Lucy is still wearing the goofy bonnet, and Dillon gets Julia's attention and, with great exaggeration, mouths the word *bonnet*. Then he giggles, and she giggles, and then he elbows Tara to clue her in on the joke, and she giggles. If there was ever such a thing as an *OMG* moment, this was it, and they knew the image of Lucy and her bonnet would be one they would savor again and again! "Selfie with Lucy!"

Lucy doesn't disappoint when she scrunches her face and bites into the jug's cork to yank it out, and now Dillon regrets he hadn't waited a minute to shoot a video instead of the selfie picture. The Winter Apple Cider Ceremony proceeds with Lucy awkwardly overfilling the first glass. She hands it to Ma, who calmly sloshes an inch or so of cider onto the ground at her side before she asks, "Who wants to taste it?" Tara's hand shoots up. "I do, I do, I do."

It is obvious to the others that Lucy has been trained to keep one eye on Ma at all times, so when the gesture comes for her to hand the glass to Tara, she obeys. Tara plays along with the ritual and swishes the cider around in her mouth and holds her glass up to the firelight to assess its clarity and pretends to smell its bouquet. She is the diner and Lucy, the sommelier. She takes a delicate sip, followed by a long, pensive, and dramatic pause and finally pronounces, "Delicious!" Then she takes a big, sloppy gulp, and they all have a good laugh.

At Ma's prompt, Lucy serves the other three. This time the cider doesn't spill over the tops, but she does fill them dangerously close to their rims, and the guests have to handle them delicately so they don't spill on their clothes. With the serving portion of her job description completed, Lucy performs a stiff curtsy and then fills a paper cup and hands it to Ma. "For me? Land sakes! How wicked! Oh well, maybe just a sip." She winks devilishly at the others.

"Here's to us getting together again and to Ma and to a wonderful time on their beautiful farm, our new home for the weekend!"

Dillon's toast causes Ma to blush a bit. "Why, that might be the kindest ol' thing anybody's said to me in a long time. It jus warms my ol' heart when our guests feel at home."

Tara just remembers something and blurts, "Hey, Ma, I meant to ask you. Our friend Shelly Roberts was supposed to come yesterday. Have you heard from her?"

Ma tilts her head up when she wants to appear smart, or at least when she wants people to believe she's thinking really hard. "Missus Roberts from Washington, DC? Yes, she came out here last year 'bout this time. I believe she's the one that made the reservations for y'all, wasn't she? You know, she did call to ask if it wuz OK to bring her baby boy out with her. Sumthin' 'bout gettin' a sitter. Lucas 'n' Lucy even dug out his ol' crib to put in her room for the baby. We expected her yesterday, but I dunno what happened. Must a got tied up or sumthin'." Ma tops off each glass with the practiced hand of an innkeeper. "But she did pay us."

"Hmm. Odd she didn't tell me." Tara feels a little hurt and turns her face down to stare into her cider. "I was really looking forward to spending time with her again. I wonder what happened."

"When you're a mother with young 'uns, ya never know what's gonna come down the pike. Things probably just got a bit complicated, that's all. I wouldn't worry too much about Missus Roberts and her baby. They'll probably show up. If y'all excuse me now, I must see to our other guests."

"What a sweet lady." Dillon's eyes follow Ma for a moment. Then pausing a bit for dramatic effect with his back to the flames, he raises his glass to the crowd. "To Shelly. Even though you can't be with us this tonight, thanks for turning us on to Winter's Farm and Orchard. Here's hoping you'll show up tomorrow."

The three raise their glasses and nod their heads in solidarity for Shelly, and the tribute continues when Tara rises and assumes Dillon's position as speaker of the tribe. "To Shelly. One thing for sure—you were right about the cider!" Everyone laughs. There's universal kudos from everyone but Julia, who hasn't touched hers.

"Wait, did you even try it?" Josh asks.

"I will."

"Jules, you have to try some."

"I will!"

Josh glares at her, hinting with every bit of body language he can muster that she should try it *now*, and she ignores him. Then he becomes more direct. "Jules, come on. You're being rude."

"I *will*." Their bickering requires everyone else to focus on them now. Julia, as usual, looks like she's about to cry, but in an uncharacteristic break from his codependency, Josh ignores her and turns to Ma, eager to let her know that at least everyone else was enjoying her homemade cider. "Can I buy some of this? I've got some buddies back home who will go nuts over this."

"Of course, honey. Lucy'll fetch a couple jugs for you and bring 'em by yer room. The more people that try our cider, the better. Like the kids say these days, 'We want it to be a virus.'"

Nobody corrects her malapropism, but Josh smiles at Ma and then Lucy. "Thanks, Lucy." She's clearly smitten by the little bit of attention Josh has just given her, and her little puppy-love gaze evolves into a stare that again lasts much longer than is comfortable. Everyone notices, but it's Ma who moves to signal that it's time to leave. She has to clear her throat when Lucy misses her cue and lingers.

"Ahem, Sweetpea . . ." Lucy snaps out of the spell, lurches forward, and gives Josh another inappropriate hug. Then she puts her head down, stomps her foot, and scampers away like a six-year-old, the cork still in her mouth. "Y'all will have to pardon my Sweetpea. She's at that stage, you know—a little boy crazy."

Tara and Julia and Dillon all share the same look of disbelief and horror as they mouth the words *boy crazy*. Josh laughs so hard he spits out a little cider, and the sight of him triggers uncontrollable laughter. Lucy is definitely the gift that keeps on giving.

"Did I miss a joke?" Ma asks.

Josh deftly covers his rudeness. "No. Um, we were just laughing at Dillon. He can get a little boy crazy too," he says, nodding his head toward Dillon.

"Ha. Ha." Dillon sarcastically plays along. Ma offers a polite smile and tries to leave.

"Would you like me to walk you back, ma'am?" Dillon offers.

"Oh, sweetie, I'm fine out here. You don't need to worry about Ma. I've been taking care of this place since long before y'all was born," she laughs, "and no harm's a come to me yet!"

Dillon laughs too. "I hope I can end up at a place like this someday with kids of my own. You are living my dream."

Ma smiles and winks at Dillon before turning to the rest of the group. "Have a good time, y'all. There's plenty of cider if ya want more and plenty of quilts I can bring over." Ma turns and disappears behind the fire.

"Why'd you say that, Josh?" Julia gets confrontational again. "That wasn't funny."

"What are you talking about?" Tempers flare again, and Dillon and Tara watch like spectators, separated from the actual event. Their sniping was, at first, a little entertaining, but over the years, it has worn a little thin, and now it's just plain tiresome. Everyone is sick of it.

"Would you two stop? We only have two nights together, and I'd like to enjoy them if we can."

"I am trying to have a good time, but someone won't let me." Before he can go on, Tara speaks up again.

"OK, no need to act like six-year-olds. You two have fought so much that Dillon and I have barely had a chance to speak to either of you. I've missed you guys."

"You're right, Tara. We are being selfish. I'm sorry. Here's to old friends." They tip their souvenir glasses toward each other, and when Josh reaches over to clink Julia's, she hesitates but ultimately gives in and returns the clink.

# 8

Ma and Pa added the bonfire to the menu of activities at Winter's Farm and Orchard by accident. At the end of a long, crisp fall day about twenty-five years ago, there had been some people picking apples at their orchard. There had been practically no wind, and since most of the visitors had already left, Pa figured nobody would notice or care if he burned some trash that had accumulated on the burn pile over on the other side of the parking lot. It had turned out there was more trash than he'd originally thought, and the fire had ended up being huge and had shot high up into the late afternoon sky. He'd been poking at it with a long stick for a while and daydreaming a bit, when his reverie had been interrupted by the sounds of *oohs* and *ahs* coming from fifteen or twenty folks sitting nearby on the grass, mesmerized by the fire. He remembers they all acted like they'd never seen fire before.

"If idiots can get all excited about watching a pile of trash burning, maybe we're onto something," he announced to Ma, and that evening, their unnamed farm officially became known as Winter's Farm and Orchard, a vanguard in a popular and developing movement that would one day be called agritourism.

As cities become more and more congested and with families increasing reluctant to let their children wander the streets at night, the lure of woods and fields, star-filled skies, and a roaring bonfire never failed to keep their occupancy rate high. And the bonfire concept was genius. Where else can people have permission to play with fire? Weekend nights were booked solid with groups and families, eager to get back to nature, and they'd go through marshmallows and Hershey Bars by the case.

A circle of ancient fieldstones set the fire pit's boundaries, and the wood came from the endless renewable resource of trees that would get toppled by fierce winds each year during one storm or another. Some guests would beg to help cut the logs, and after that, they'd want to haul and stack them near the fire pit. They'd even stoke the fire to keep it going. For some of the guests, it was reliving a past memory; for others it was creating a new one. But to Ma and Pa, it was easy money from an easy formula: let the paying guests do most of the work by keeping them a little buzzed on their famous apple cider.

And tonight, the fire was keeping people warm and the cider was keeping them laughing. "Oh my god, the guy with the hook hand gets me every time," Tara admits with a little shiver. Ghost stories. There's something about the camaraderie of sitting around a fire with friends and strangers and a little alcohol that makes the old ones exciting and even chilling again. "But doesn't he get his hook caught on their car bumper just before they ride off?" corrects Julia at the completion of a tale told by another guest.

"Oh come on, Jules. Who cares? Go with the flow!" Josh slurs. "Let's have another jug of cider. Oh, bartender!"

"Josh!" Julia scolds. "I think you've had enough." Tara shoots Julia a cold stare. Julia's face asks "What? Why are you looking at me like that?"

"Fun's over, I guess," she snaps. "Time to watch you two fight again like you're on trashy cable."

# 9

Dillon is desperate to keep everyone engaged, but Josh and Julia's little flare up has temporarily put a damper on the fun. "Hey, then there's the one where friends huddle around a bonfire in the middle of a field near the edge of a wood. They all take turns spinning yarns and telling ghost stories. One of them tells a real creepy story he swears up and down is true. It's quiet except for the crackling of the fire, and then somebody steps into view and clears their throat. Do you guys remember that one? It was such a great story, but I forget what happens after that." Nobody responds. Now that the fire is burning lower, they've all drifted into silence, and they're just staring at the coals.

There's a clunking sound when a couple more logs are thrown on the fire, and the snapping and popping and crackling of the new wood is so loud they almost don't catch the sound of a newcomer, when she steps into view and clears her throat. The guttural sound is followed by an *ahem*, courtesy of a batty-looking middle-aged woman who has emerged presumably from the other side of the bonfire. "Excuse me," she asks weakly. "May I join you?"

"Yes! That's it! You're my story!" cries Dillon, giving Tara a high-five.

Josh turns his head toward the stranger with minimal interest. "Huh?"

"Never mind, Josh. You had to have paid attention."

The lady moves a step toward them and takes a deep breath—for courage, maybe—because she seems a little panicked. She's also really a fright. Her long gray hair is piled up high and messy, held together with those chopstick-like things so popular in the sixties. Everything she's wearing has polka dots, including a polka-dot scarf and a matching polka-dot beret. She takes off her hat to speak, "Really, do you mind? I'd like to sit with you."

"Um, sure. OK, I guess," responds Tara, looking around at the others for support.

"Are you serious? Absolutely, sit right here next to me, young lady," kids Dillon, always looking for some adventure. "The name's Dillon. What's on your mind?"

"I'm alone here, and I was watching you for a while to be sure you were nice people. I feel I need a little protection, so I'd like to stay nearby, if you don't mind."

Tara likes to say she just speaks her truth. In front of her, friends explain her outbursts by saying she lacks that valve most people have that limits the outflow of inappropriate behavior. Behind her back, though, most will agree she is often just a bitch.

"Um, look, lady. You seem nice enough, but we're four old friends who haven't seen each other for a while, and we'd kind of like to do that. No offense." The other three were stunned at how measured she was.

"Oh, I understand, and I'm not asking to be part of your group. If I could just literally stay next to your group until we all go back to the house, I'd feel a lot safer. I'm Carrie, by the way."

"Her name would be Carrie," Tara mutters under her breath.

Julia jumps in now and adds, "Carrie, please stay with us as long as you want. Just know that some of us have been drinking a bit, and well . . . as long as you know what you're getting into."

"So what makes you need protection, Carrie?" Dillon is fascinated by this new creature who seems to have fallen from the sky. "Was it the guy with the hook arm?" he chuckles. "You know that one gets me every time." He can't help staring at her outfit. "Nice hat, by the way."

"Oh, thanks. I like polka dots. It's kind of my trademark, I guess."

"Yes, well, polka dots are so timeless," a sarcastic Tara mutters, looking at Julia.

It was kismet that placed these two ardent fashionistas in the same dorm room their freshman year at Georgetown University, and it was their family money that kept them in style. In Julia's case, her innate fashion sense was more than a little superficial character trait; it ended up leading her to a career in an entire industry based on superficiality. After completing her degree in comparative literature, she moved to New York to pursue another degree in fashion design at Parsons and with that under her stylish belt, she was able to parlay her job as a grunt in a design house into a career as a successful stylist. For a couple of crazy years, she traveled the world on one photo shoot or another, until she fell madly for an up-and-coming lawyer with an MBA and moved with him to Washington, DC.

Washington had never been much of a fashion capital, so for a while she was happily married but unhappily unemployed. Freelancing remained an easy option, but most of that work was still happening in New York, and the commute was taking its toll on their relationship. In the past year or so, she thought she'd take a stab at writing fiction, but it was too soon to tell how it would turn out because she hadn't managed to write a thing.

Tara's passion for style and fashion was baked in and assumed a large role in her personality. It was an odd mix, though, because she considered herself pretty much a math nerd and a stunning, beautiful one at that. After Georgetown, she earned her terminal degree in applied mathematics at MIT and was smart and lucky enough to get a tenure track position on the faculty. In spite of all her liberal sophistication and training in logic, though, her old superficial prejudices quite often take control, and right now she can't believe Carrie really isn't what she's wearing. *Holy crap, are those polka-dot socks, too?*

"So you didn't answer me. What are you afraid of, Carrie?" repeats Dillon.

Carrie brings her voice down to a whisper. "Okay. So listen, all of you. It's important you understand everything. There is some stuff going on here that is very troubling. First of all, in full disclosure, let me confess that I'm operating undercover." She pauses and looks around at her audience. Even in the dark they can see that Carrie is one of those people who sometimes talks with her eyes closed. They flutter open only briefly tonight, and though the group finds that habit annoying, they listen with pretend respectfulness. It does, however, make it easier for them to exchange sarcastic facial expressions.

"I'm a journalist, a freelancer, and . . ." Dillon is starting his famous eye roll that never fails to crack up Tara, and it is all she could do to keep from sputtering out a big laugh. "Actually, I hope to start a blog soon. I like to think I'm a bit of an amateur sleuth too, and I've been digging into a pattern of disappearances out here. Each one starts out with a big story, but in every case, the leads dry up and the stories never go anywhere. I've been staying in the bed-and-breakfasts out here to see what I could find out, and what I found out was that all signs point here. Nobody in the Winter family will say they know anything at all about any of the disappearances—at least they pretend not to know anything. But since I've been here, I've found out quite a lot, and it's all upstairs in my room."

"And what did you find out about, exactly?"

"I'm getting to that." Her delivery style seems studied or at least rehearsed. Points she thinks relevant or crucial she punctuates with dramatic pauses. "Yesterday"—pause—"a nice woman"—pause—"another guest"—pause—"arrived here during the day about the same time I did. I thought she looked nice, and when I saw her coming down for dinner, I asked if we could sit together. We had only spoken a couple seconds when she apologized and said she had to run straight back to her room. She was very vague about the reason, so I followed her up the stairs and asked if we could then maybe together *after* dinner. That wasn't good for her either, so I said I'd see her at breakfast in the morning, *this* morning."

Tara is making an "I told you so" expression to the others.

"You might not believe me, and I don't blame you, but there were several people there at the time—well, not on the stairway of course—but it will be easy to prove in a court of law, and we won't have any trouble getting plenty of witnesses when the time comes."

Everyone is now looking at everyone else. *Huh? Court of law? When the time comes? What is she talking about?*

In lieu of a pause, this time Carrie's head darts right and left and back right again, as if to be certain no one was there before she continued, "And this morning she didn't show up."

By now all four were stealing quick looks at each other and joining Dillon in the eye rolling but otherwise pretending to listen. Tara was digging her elbow into his ribs, and the two could hardly keep from laughing. Josh can't stand it any longer. "Why are you whispering?"

Carrie is oblivious to the sarcasm and continues, "She just disappeared. I went to her room and knocked on the door for a long time. She didn't answer, so she couldn't have been in her room, or she would have answered, right? Since the house is old and the locks are old too, I got creative and peeked through the keyhole. It was probably wrong, but I'd seen Miss Marple do it once. Anyway, I saw that her stuff was still in the room. Odd, right? I know it sounds far-fetched, but there are other things going on around here that make me suspect. she's just the latest in a string of disappearances and . . ." Carrie pauses and looks around again before whispering, "Murders."

"Murders? Murders? Who's doing the murdering? Ma? Pa? Lucy?" Tara's limiting valve was not functioning because she blurted it out so loudly everyone around the fire stopped to stare and listen.

"Shh! We can't let them know we know. If they think we know, we could all be in danger! And I'll tell you why. I've got it all figured out." This time, as she looks to one side, her eyes grow gigantic and her face freezes in terror. Ma has materialized out of nowhere, and against the backdrop of the roaring bonfire, her sturdy frame looms like an action figure. As Carrie scrambles to get up, she trips over the hem of her long peasant dress and falls down spread-eagle between Ma and the fire.

"Oh, glory! I didn't mean to scare y'all. Just came to see if you folks needed anything. Don't mean to be a bother," Ma apologizes, and with one strong motion, she grabs Carrie's arm and yanks her to her feet, perhaps a little more forcibly than is required. "Sorry, dearie."

With her bearings intact, Carrie backs off and slinks into the shadows again. Julia is glad Ma has come back. "We're great, thanks."

"Just great? This is the most fun I've had in ages," adds Dillon. "Who's that woman, and how do you find such fascinating guests?" He turns to Tara for confirmation and whispers, "Did you see the look Ma gave her? Wow, if looks could kill."

"It means the world to hear you say that, it really does, bless your little hearts." Ma's icy look becomes all smiles, and as she nods her head back to indicate she is referencing Carrie, she starts raising her eyebrows up and down like Groucho Marx. "Now that guest wuzn't bothering you now, wuz she?"

"No, not at all," Tara mumbles. "She was a little weird, though."

"So should we all be afraid of you, Ma? That lady thinks you murdered a guest yesterday, or maybe this morning." Everyone laughs, and Dillon holds up his glass as Ma pours him more cider.

Ma giggles, "So now I'm a murderer, am I?" Then she cups her hand and pretends to whisper privately to the group, "Pa an' me think she just might be a little *off*." She does her eyebrow thing again just to ensure everyone is on the same page with her.

"A *little* off?" They all get the joke and burst into laughter.

"I thought it wuz maybe getting a little chilly, so I brought you these quilts. You can share." Ma winks before turning to leave.

Josh feels the need to take charge of the group, and he stands up to face them all. "OK, now. Can we all agree if that crazy lady comes back, we blow her off?"

Tara nods. "Definitely!"

"Are you kidding? I love her," adds Dillon, "and I'm gonna be her new best friend tonight."

Julia bewilders the others by suggesting she'd actually like to hear what Carrie has to say, and Josh glares at her for breaking ranks, but before he has a chance to open his mouth, she preempts him. "Why not?"

"Well, because we'll be opening a big ol' Pandora's box of crazy here, that's why."

"Stop," Julia commands. "Don't be an ass."

"Hey, Josh is right, the other woman could tell right away. No wonder she ran up the stairs back to her room. She even gave up her dinner, though I doubt she went to all the trouble of getting herself murdered just to avoid her." Everyone has a good laugh.

"Undercover? Amateur sleuth whatever? Blogger? Miss Marple? What part of crazy didn't you get? You can have her, Dillon, she's all yours, but that means she'll have to sit with you too."

A little while later Carrie reappears. Her eyes dart back and forth and behind her and then horizontally again, like a comic's caricature of a paranoid person. She dabs her forehead with her scarf. "The kids are all spies, you know, and they're all over the place. It's too late to get together tonight, but tomorrow morning we'll talk and I'll fill you in. I'll think of a safe place where we can meet." She's still looking around, afraid someone is nearby, listening.

"Yes, a safe place, by all means." No one knows to respond, and once again, Tara takes the lead. "That's awfully nice of you, but we already have plans for tomorrow."

"You'll have to change your plans. This is too important. For us all."

"Huh?" Josh reacts quickly, but he says what everyone is thinking.

"I said you'll have to change your plans. Don't you understand the danger we're all in?"

Josh tries again, "Actually no, I don't think we do understand."

"OK, so now when you say *the danger we're all in* you mean like the murder thing, right?" Tara's sarcasm is relentless.

"So, Carrie, what's going on between you and Ma, anyway? I thought you said you were a guest. I mean, she certainly doesn't treat you like one. What in the world did you do to her?"

"Well, you see, this is the problem. I'm pretty sure she knows I know too much, and I think she's out to get me."

Tara mumbles, "Yeah. Um, okay."

Now Julia looks at Carrie. "What did that lady look like? How old? Our age? Did you catch her name?"

"What lady?"

"You know the woman you told us about that you had trouble connecting with."

"Oh, I didn't get her name, but I don't know, I guess she was about your age, maybe. It was hard to tell. She talked with kind of an accent, though."

"What kind of an accent?"

"I don't know exactly, like she might be from the East."

"What do you mean *the East*? Like China?"

"No, not the East like China. East like New York or New Jersey or someplace like that."

"Could you remember if she said her name was Shelly?" Julia persists.

"I'm not sure. Yeah, maybe something like that. I don't really know. Why?"

Tara whispers into Dillon's ear, "Some super sleuth. Didn't pick up a thing."

"Because our friend Shelly was supposed to join us here, but she hasn't shown up, and Ma says she never did."

"Of course she would say that. See what I mean? This is all worse than I thought."

"With all due respect, I don't see how you think Shelly could possibly be involved in all this intrigue." Tara wishes the woman would just go away.

Julia prods further. "What time? What time do we meet you tomorrow?"

"Seven thirty," Carrie states firmly.

"Huh? You are joking, right?"

"All right." Carrie an see her early call was not well recived. "We'll make it nine, but nine sharp. We don't have any time to lose. My room."

No, wait—too obvious. Make it the dining room, where we'll all be out in the open. I mean, what could they do to us there?"

"Good grief," Tara mutters.

Ma reappears again with the enthusiasm of the games coordinator on a cruise ship. "Say, I wuz wondering if you folks would fancy a whirl on our famous moonlight hayride. We've almost got a full wagon."

"Is it scary?" Tara worries.

Now it's Ma's turn to look over her shoulder to be sure she isn't heard. She lowers her voice and winks conspiratorially, as though she doesn't want what she's about to tell them to go any farther. "Let me tell you, folks out here go on 'n' on 'bout how it's the scariest hayride they've ever been on. But thems just the ones that live to tell about it, ha-ha. An' the rest? Well, we never see or hear from 'em ever agin." The last part she delivers with the solemnity of a professional storyteller at the conclusion of a Grimm tale. All she lacks is the big book to close shut at the end.

"Sure, we're in," Tara leads, "right?" She looks around for confirmation.

"Absolutely!" Dillon agrees.

"I'm down," Josh says too.

Julia remains quiet and predictably not enthused. "Why don't you all go ahead? I'll just head back to our room."

A tipsy Tara is determined not to allow Julia's bad mood to dominate the mood of the whole group. "Jules. Stop it. Am I going to have to make all the decisions for you? The hayride is famous, and it's going to be fun. Look, I can tell you're still thinking about the crazy lady. Forget about that kook. It couldn't have been Shelly anyway, because Ma said she never checked in. Jeez."

"What did I do this time?" Ma blurts with a smile.

"Oh, hey everyone, don't you get it? I figured it out. The bonfire, the ghost stories." Dillon can't resist giggling, and he points with his thumb in the direction Carrie went a few minutes ago. "And crazy Carrie. They're all set up for the hayride, right, Ma?"

"Well, I declare I'm sure I don't know what y'all are talking about." Ma's eyes twinkle, and she giggles back like a schoolgirl. "What kind of wild notions did that Masterson woman fill y'all's heads with now?"

"Oh, nothing much, just that we are all in really, really serious danger and that she had figured it all out and had things to tell us that just can't wait, you know, and stuff like that. We played along and said we'd meet with her in the morning. She was something else," said Tara. "I hope you're paying her plenty."

Dillon pipes up, "I never expected any of this. Did you know about the hayride, Josh? I feel like we're in a movie."

Ma puts on her serious face for a minute and spends a minute milking her audience. "Gimme a minute to tell Pa we've got more takers an' I'll be back. A movie now, land sakes alive."

As soon as she deems it safe, Carrie rejoins the group. "I don't know about this," she confides quietly to Dillon.

"Don't worry, we'll all be on the hayride together." Then for the benefit of Tara, he adds, "You can sit next to me."

"Let's go." Ma is back and claps her hands to signal she's in charge. She raises her hand high in the air so people can see to follow her, reminding Tara of all the tour guides she'd see with pink umbrellas and other goofy things they use to keep their groups together. Tonight she wants to think of the right prop for Ma to use for her hayride—a pitchfork, maybe, or some other farm implement.

"Lead on, Ma," shouts Josh. He's pretty buzzed and eager for the next adventure.

* * *

On any given school day in September and October, up to seven or eight school busses will line the driveway of Winter's Farm and Orchard, each one bringing elementary schoolchildren from about six surrounding counties. Teachers like bringing their classes to the farm because the field trips are very well-organized and they don't have to do much. School administrators like the setup because they know the Winters include an academic class activity to comply with the state regulations for these trips. Ma has her own dedicated group of capable teachers and eager assistants who teach kids how pumpkins grow and how to navigate a corn maze. They also are responsible for the important logistics of moving the vast numbers of students from activity to activity. The kids have such a good time with on their class trip many return with their parents on the weekends for more fun.

The hayride is, by far, the most popular part of the field trip. The festive hay wagon follows a winding and bumpy loop around the farm, and colorful Pumpkin People scarecrows dressed to represent characters from fairy tales entertain the kids along the way. It's fun, it's outdoors, it's interactive—if not a little cheesy—but everyone knows it's good and it's wholesome.

*Wholesome* is not a word that would ever be used to describe their nighttime hayride, which is part of what Ma and Pa called their haunting season. Because it was off-limits to children under a certain age, getting to go on that hayride had become somewhat a rite of passage for hundreds of kids, and each year, a new crop of kids now one year older and eager to experience its thrills would look forward to making the cut. But the cutoff age was largely a myth. Ma set the policy, and because she often couldn't remember what her policy was, it varied from week to week and year to year. She called herself the Decider and stood at the head of the line, where she would tell each child whether they were "in" or "out."

# 10

**P**a's rough, calloused hands help steady the thirty-odd passengers up the steep and rickety steps up the old-fashioned hay wagon. For seating, square hay bales line the wooden fence like railings that make the sides. The fresh and pungent aroma of the extra hay covering the floor in the center of the wagon adds pleasant authenticity to the atmosphere. A good whiff of Pa's boozy breath provides an element of danger.

The tall and ancient John Deere tractor with its rusted smokestack and pipes sticking out of everywhere is reminiscent of a Norman Rockwell painting. It looks like one of those contraptions that would be difficult to start, but with its huge wheels as tall as Pa, it appears to be more than up to the task of pulling a hayride wagon full of adults. After the last passenger has safely boarded, Pa returns to the tractor to assume his post as designated driver. During Ma's spiel to the wagon full of passengers, he has just enough time to roll another cigarette.

Ma uses her flashlight on the hay wagon like an usher seating spectators in a dark theater, but unlike typical directives to concertgoers, she encourages her audience to "squeeze together and get cozy." Tara and Dillon find two bales next to each other and huddle under one of the quilts they brought along from the bonfire. Josh and Julia share another quilt, but they are conspicuously not huddling.

When it is her turn to climb aboard, a nervous Carrie avoids eye contact with Ma. She tries to be as inconspicuous as possible when she slides unobtrusively onto the hay bale next to Dillon, but Ma is quick to flash her light to an empty seat on the other side of the wagon and bark, "Missus Masterson, why don't you sit over there?" It isn't really a question at all but more of a command. To soften it, she adds, "You know, for balance." As she stands up to move to the other side, Carrie shares a look of terror with Dillon, who responds by lifting up his hands to mime that he doesn't understand either. Then he gives her a big reassuring smile. "I guess it's like flying on one of those small planes," he shouts. "They shift people around all the time." Then he notices Ma giving Pa what looks to be some kind of hand signal. "Uh-oh. I see another setup. This is going to be good."

"Are we all first timers out here?" Most people raise their hands and nod, but one couple yells out they've been on it before. "I don't know what you've heard, but I reckon y'all wouldn't be here if you didn't know what you wuz getting into. Our hayride's famous for a reason, and it'll speak for it itself. But I can tell y'all that you can holler as loud as you want. Out here, ain't no one can hear ya scream." People pretend to chuckle. "Y'all have fun now," she adds as she clicks off her light. "Remember to stay in your seats! Safety first. We don't want nobody to get hurt. An' whatever happens, don't get off the wagon!" Pa cranks up the tractor engine and grinds it into gear. The wagon lurches forward into the darkness to the clanking and clashing together of the chains and pins securing their connections with the tractor.

"Come on, closer to me," Josh tells Julia, lifting his left arm for her to cuddle under it.

"Josh, I'm fine. I think I can take care of myself on a hayride." She turns to look over the railing to see where they are going. Josh looks defeated, but she doesn't notice.

The tractor route takes the wagon along the edge of the woods, where some of the older and taller tree branches are low enough for some of the people to touch. It's been about five minutes, and so far nothing interesting has happened. Since nothing is happening, the passengers start to become disgruntled, and they talk amongst themselves. From the gist of their conversations, most agree the famous Haunting Season Hayride is not living up to the hype. On the contrary, it's been a big bust and seems to be getting worse. From one of those low-hanging branches ahead on the left hangs a cartoonish scarecrow with a burlap scarecrow head. Its smile was made with a magic marker and is anything but magical. A couple other scarecrows off to the left are supposed to look menacing, but like the first one, they're a little lame. Then from behind a tree comes an unconvincing moan, probably from a teenager. Tara and Dillon look at each other in disbelief and disappointment. *Seriously?*

An actor in a dollar-store Spiderman mask leaps out from the tree line. "Boo!" he shouts halfheartedly, and Dillon and Tara can't help themselves—they start cracking up. "Spiderman isn't supposed to be evil and scare people. Can't they do better than this?"

"I could barely even hear him over the tractor," Tara laughs.

"I know," says Dillon. "What was he—like twelve?"

Carrie crosses the wagon again to sit next to Julia and whispers in her ear, "I can tell things have changed. It simply can't wait. My room is almost all the way down the hall on the right. It's easy to find, because it's the only room with a wreath hanging on the door. Meet me there tonight after the hayride. Come as late as you want. I'm always up, and everything I want to show you is there."

Julia glances around. No one's paying attention to their conversation, because they are all holding their own conversations. They need to speak directly into each other's ears and use lots of gestures to communicate over the loud rattling of the tractor. Carrie pleads with Julia again, "Promise you'll come. If anything happens to me, call the police. And don't trust the Winters, any of them! Promise!"

Julia is confused. Carrie is keeping a watchful eye all around her. She looks to the woods and forward toward Pa every few seconds, and Julia can't tell if she's searching for something or afraid of the hayride, just plain kooky, or as Dillon maintains, a bad actor in a good role.

The wagon plods on in its monotonous way from the dark but inconsequential trail into thicker and more sinister woods. To the right is the tall and imposing outside wall of a cornfield, and it's right about there, far from the lights of the farmhouse and far from anything, that the tractor engine unexpectedly coughs and sputters to a halt. Everyone groans, "Oh no! Now what? Really?" Some suggest it's part of the hayride. Carrie cringes when she sees Pa hop off the tractor. He throws up the hood to inspect, and smoke billows out. Everyone looks to the couple who said they'd been on it before.

"Is this it? Was it like this last year? No, it couldn't have been, or you wouldn't have come back, would you?"

"No, it's usually real scary and fun," they insist. "And the tractor never broke down before. But they say the hayride changes every year, so we don't really know."

Pa flips on his flashlight, and when he shines it back toward the wagon, it catches Carrie scooting back to her assigned bale. Then with his trusty cigarette dangling from his nicotine-stained lips, he turns back to poke around the engine with his flashlight, presumably looking for a telltale explanation for the breakdown.

"Wait, seriously? I thought this was supposed to be scary," someone says among the growing chorus of boos and hisses. To make a better assessment of the situation, Tara leans her upper body out over the wagon's side railing and cranes to see what's happening with the tractor. After a moment, she jumps to her feet and addresses the crowd, "I'll tell you what's scaring me—it's Pa's lit cigarette so close to the motor! I don't know about the rest of you, but I think I've seen enough. Anyone want to head back with me?"

A few people stand up tentatively. Someone *gently* points out Ma had said not to get off the wagon, no matter what happens. Tara ignores the warning. "Well, that's not a problem, nothing's happening!" She's about to jump down off the wagon, when a *rip* from the woods freezes her in place. The second *rip* is louder and more menacing, and it's getting closer to the wagon. "Yay, a chainsaw! I knew there had to be one!" somebody else shouts. Others aren't quite as happy to see a lumbering brute in a Leatherface mask stumble out from the woods brandishing a huge chainsaw in his massive arms.

"Holy shit!" Tara plops back down on her bale. The ones who had been squealing in delight at the sound of the first chainsaw are now shouting in terror, and when Leatherface jumps up onto the railing, people from his side of the wagon react by piling onto the floor in the center for safety.

"It's about time this got . . . whoa!" Josh doesn't finish speaking before another chainsaw roars up from beneath the wagon! This one is wielded by a big creepy clown, who scales the other side of the wagon, causing everyone from that side to scramble to the center too, adding more arms and more legs to the existing snarl. Teenage girls scream, and hay flies everywhere as the chainsaws tear through wood searching for flesh. Not one person is laughing now.

The Clown and Leatherface jump down onto the wagon floor, and everyone from the pile flees back to the relative safety of their hay bales. Leatherface grabs what looks to be the skinny teenage boyfriend of a very terrified girl and drags him down the steps, off the wagon and into the woods. They boy puts up a pretty good fight, but Leatherface is much bigger and stronger. His girlfriend is sitting next to Julia on the other side, and she does her best at pretending to cry. Then the Clown, starting at one end of the wagon, sniffs at the passengers all the way along to the front. He spins around and stomps back to the middle of the wagon, where he grabs a frightened Carrie and throws her over his shoulders fireman-style.

"Help, help! They're going to kill me! Help! Help me!" There is some hysterical laughter mixed with the screams from the crowd.

The Clown lugs his frantic victim the length of the wagon back toward the steps, and as she passes Julia, their wide eyes lock. By now the chopsticks have been knocked off her head, and large bunches of her thick and now unmanaged hair clump and droop over her eyes. Looking like a wicked witch in a choke hold, she points one frail arm in Julia's direction and yells out in a raspy voice, "Shelly!"

Most people react with screams or nervous laughter. "Oh my lord," a lady passenger moans, fearing she could be next. Her husband grabs her hand and tries to comfort her. "It's all part of the show. It's all part of the show. It's all part of the show." But Dillon, Tara, and Josh are having a great time of it. "Man, she was good!" jokes Josh. Julia, meanwhile, is paralyzed. As one by one the guests untangle themselves and retake their seats on the hay bales, there's lots of buzzing and gasping and recapping. One kid can't stop bawling, but the agony becomes ecstasy again when they realize how just how much fun they had.

But in the new quiet, they notice the wagon isn't moving. It's still parked in the dark and in the middle of nowhere. A chainsaw rips again from the woods where Leatherface dragged the boy, and that sound is followed immediately by a bloodcurdling but masculine scream. "Shel-ly!" Then quiet again. While everyone was focused on what horrible thing must be going on out to the left, there's another *rip* from the cornfield, where the Clown had dragged Carrie. Heads snap to the right, and a different but equally realistic and higher-pitched scream sounds like "Shel-ly."

"What the fu—?" Tara is so into this.

The angry chainsaw rips violently again, but this one continues screeching for another couple of minutes, and there are no further human screams. Then the motor peters out and goes quiet. It's over. Dead silence comes from the cornfield.

"Shelly? Who's Shelly?" someone asks.

"That's me. I'm Shelly. I'm his girlfriend," says the woman, pointing with her thumb at the spot next to her where the guy had sat before he'd gotten dragged from the wagon. She tries to say it straight-faced, but she's not much of an actor, and when she can't help snickering, everyone gets a good laugh. The people next to her pat her on the back and congratulate both of them for a job well done.

Pa slams the hood, adding a huge crash to the cacophony, and now everyone's focus shifts back to the wagon. He mounts the tractor seat, and the engine roars back to life. "All fixed!" he announces, grinning over his shoulder. He throws the tractor into gear, and the hay wagon jerks forward again on its journey.

"Great show!" Tara shouts to Pa, who just drives on ahead, ignoring her.

"Josh, did I or did I not totally call Polka Dots being in on it?" Dillon boasts about his premonition.

"Yeah, yeah. You keep saying that, but I knew what was going to happen all along. You could tell when . . ."

"Bullshit, Josh. I saw your face when Leatherface pulled that first dude away. You were all . . ." Tara mocks him by imitating the expression he must have worn. "Yeah, there, that's it! That's the face you made!" she teases. Josh's face is filled with terror, but he's not pretending. He grabs her shoulders and twists her around, putting her face-to-face with the Clown, who had climbed back up on the railing behind her. He's holding two severed and bloody heads by the hair. Now it's back to the center of the wagon, as people pile on top of each other again. This time, though, it seems more urgent. The Clown hangs onto the back of the wagon rail with one arm, like a garbage collector hanging on to the back of his truck, and the two freakish heads dangle from his free hand. He swings them forward and backward, bashing them against the railing of the wagon, spraying blood and teeth onto the passengers. For the two or three of them who have their eyes open, he's putting on quite a show. It will be a long time before they'll be able to forget the sound of skulls cracking watching those bloody jaws opening and closing on that bumpy and horrifying ride from hell.

Julia freaks out. The more she screams, the tighter Josh hugs her. "Jules, it's okay. It's not real, baby. It's not real."

Then he turns to Tara. "How the hell did they do that, Tara?"

"Josh, really?"

Nobody noticed exactly when the Clown leaves their hay wagon, but when they open their eyes again and the tractor is huffing and puffing toward its stop at the entrance to the corn maze, he is gone. A smiling Ma is standing to greet them amid kudos like "Amazing!" "Unbelievable!" "*So much better than last year's hayride, way more realistic!*"

By now, most everyone can't wait to get off the hay wagon. Some chatter nervously as they wobble down the steps, and others stop at the bottom to give an arm to the next rattled person behind them. There is understandable apprehension about what is to come in the Scary Giant Corn Maze, and as each moment of the hayride gets retold and rehashed, recreated and reanalyzed, at least a couple people announce they've had enough for one night.

# 11

"All right, first part's over everyone." Ma elbows her way through the crowd toward the ominous entrance. Julia feels ten times better with Ma around, and in a moment of surprising and uncharacteristic familiarity, she jumps at the invitation to rest her head on Ma's huge bosom. "Come, come now, Julia dear." Ma strokes her hair sweetly with one hand and gestures with her other. "Y'all have fun in the corn maze now. Stay on the paths, and you won't get lost. We want to see y'all coming out the other end now, don't we? Be safe!"

In preparation for their treks into the maze, folks in the crowd fumble with cell phones to activate their flashlight apps. Arcs of random light appear and crisscross everywhere. "Oh, and most important of all," Ma adds. "What happens in the Corn Maze stays in the Corn Maze." Given the polite and forced laughter coming from all around, Ma knows that after a good ten years of service, it's probably time to work up a new line.

"Say, I couldn't help overhearing what you were talking about at the bonfire with that woman." One of the women makes a point of working her way through the crowd to speak to Julia. "It's probably none of my business, but you know the actor who got abducted on the hayride? Well, she was telling you the truth. We were outside the farmhouse at the same time yesterday as the lady she was talking about—you know, the one she said spoke with a New York accent or something. I remember it vividly because she was carrying an infant and my husband had wanted to help her with her bag, but he had an armful of pumpkins and couldn't. It was probably not your friend, but I just thought I'd pass it along because I know everyone thought she was a little crazy."

"Thank you. I appreciate it. But you know, I'm pretty sure it couldn't have been my friend either."

"C'mon." Josh offers Julia his hand. She smiles back, and Tara and Dillon muscle up front to join them and be the first ones in.

# 12

They change the circuitous route through the maze to the exit every year; at least that's what the farm brochure states in big, bold letters. What doesn't change, though, is how complicated it is and thus how easy it is to get lost. All the regulars say that making the right choice at the first possible junction is critical to getting out. If you are one of the unlucky ones who make that first turn wrong, you can find yourself in an endless series of twists and turns and long loops that become elaborate wild goose chases and dead ends, and you can end up back where you started, sometimes over and over again. Since the correct first turn last year was to the right, some assume this year the Winters *must* have mixed things up a bit, and they'll try to make everyone think left is right. Then again, others assume that's just what they want us to think and that the Winters will keep it the same, so left isn't the right way, but right is. And that's what makes it fun every year.

To Josh, Julia, Tara, and Dillon, the path seems pretty straightforward at the outset. There are a couple turns and a few dead ends here and there, with some circles and choices to make, but overall, it seems simple. Anyway, they don't have a system. They are so psyched and enjoy talking and laughing together so much they are deep into the maze before they realize it. Their navigation is made even easier by the light of a sliver of moon.

Josh is glad to see Julia having such a good time with Tara, and he hopes it will help stabilize her mood. It is one of the reasons he is content to lag behind them a few yards. When Josh and Dillon reach the next intersection where they can make a right or left, Dillon gives Josh a little elbow jab to the ribs. He picks up on it, and they consciously dart in the opposite direction of the gals. They kick into high gear and sprint for a minute or so to be sure they've ditched them, and they are laughing so hard they don't hear Tara and Julia begging them to come back.

"Look at the boobs on this one with the microphone." Josh has stumbled across a small grouping of pumpkin people in a small clearing. "Her name tag says *Dolly Pumpkin*." Just down from Dolly stands a blushing pumpkin bride in an ivory dress with a long train, complete with veil. Her bridal bouquet is plastic, but the groom facing her in the powder-blue tuxedo with a white ruffled shirt sports what was once a real boutonniere. After two months in the sun, it's nearly unrecognizable as a carnation. The solemn pumpkin priest reads from a small white plastic-covered copy of the New Testament.

Just past the wedding party, the path splits, but fueled by Ma's special cider, Josh and Dillon opt to barge on ahead right through the corn, breaking one of the cardinal rules of the corn maze: *Stay on the path*!

\* \* \*

The Winters generally plant the corn for their mazes in both directions. It takes double the seed to do it that way, but they end up with a maze that's twice as thick. Ma reckons that after about twenty to thirty minutes of getting lost and having fun, many people get bored or scared and they look for a quick way out. If the corn is dense, it's more difficult to get through and less tempting to try. When Ma chants her admonition to *stay on the path*, she says it to keep people from trampling down the corn to make shortcuts, which can ruin the puzzle for subsequent visitors. She also knows that the deeper a person goes off course into the corn, the more likely that person is to get lost, and lost people then need to be found.

\* \* \*

Josh and Dillon are able to bash and stomp through forty or fifty feet of thick corn before they lose interest. What began as a lark ended up being a lot more work than they had imagined, and they are about to call it quits and turn around, when Josh finds something. The moon's cycle is on the wane, and tonight, earthlings are only allowed a tiny sliver of light, but there is enough to reveal a small circle of cleared corn about fifteen feet in diameter. Josh uses the remaining bit of battery in his phone to illuminate what turns out to be a small scenario that is less elaborate but more realistic than the others they encountered.

* * *

Julia and Tara have given up on Josh and Dillon ever coming back, and they resolve to have their own fun, but the path they took when they had been abandoned soon requires them to make more decisions. They are having so much fun playing catchup they meander the paths aimlessly, making arbitrary choices instead of really navigating. Their last turn takes them into a large circular clearing, and the change in surroundings catches their attention.

"Wow, what's this?"

"I don't know, but I hope we won't have to retrace our steps to get back. I haven't a clue how we got here."

About a dozen pumpkin people populate the circle, and they are evenly spread out around the circumference like numbers on a clock face. There is enough moonlight to get the big picture, but to fully appreciate each character, they need to get closer.

"Hey, Jules, look. Here's a guy in a Sigma Chi jersey. Remember Scott? He was pretty cute, but that sweetheart thing didn't work out so well for you, did it?"

"No, I didn't keep that pin long. Thanks for reminding me. Hey, here's one from Washington and Lee University. William Woods College? How in the world did these get here?"

"Here we are, look at all the Georgetown sweatshirts. This is so cool." The pumpkin people in the collegiate section are not just wearing their school colors; they are also accessorized with props, like lacrosse sticks and catchers' mitts, though the sports doesn't necessarily match up with the school's tradition or reputation. The guy in the Peabody Conservatory sweatshirt, for example, is swinging a baseball bat.

"Is it just me," Tara asks, "or do you think it's pretty hysterical to see all these A-list schools represented here when the owners can hardly put a sentence together properly? I'll have to remember to ask Ma where they came from."

* * *

The scene Josh saw in the corner obviously is meant to look like an operating table. It consists of a six-foot-long wooden table, complete with a headless body and obligatory fake blood splattered all over the table. A bloody chainsaw sits off to the side. "Finally, something scary. Now it's getting fun."

"All they need now is a pumpkin doctor and a sexy pumpkin nurse." Dillon notices a bloody polka-dot scarf on the ground next to the table. "See! I knew I was right. The whole thing with that crazy chick was staged. We were supposed to stumble onto this."

"Selfie!" One shutter sound later and the scene becomes memorialized, but it was a mistake to lean against the table. "Crap! I think the paint's still wet. It's all over my jeans. How about you? Shit! They were good jeans."

"Yeah, I got a little on me too, I guess. We've got to come back here during the day tomorrow and see what else there is. Ma and Pa really put on a good show."

"Glad to see you having fun, man," Dillon tells him.

Josh laughs, "I just needed some away time from Julia. All the sadness wears off on me."

"That's understandable," Dillon consoles him. "It's hard to be happy when the one you love isn't happy."

"Shh! Quiet!" Josh whispers. "Do you hear something?"

They stop speaking, but Dillon responds by nodding. They both can hear the sounds of footsteps rustling through the dry cornstalks from behind the operating table. It's impossible to tell from how close or far away, but it's definitely someone tromping through the corn and not walking on a cut path.

"Hey, Ma said you're supposed to stay on the path!" Josh shouts jokingly at whoever is out in the corn. But nobody responds when the rustling stops, and it sends a little chill down his spine. Then as the person seems to head away in a different direction, the sound fades with him.

"Jeez, for a minute I forgot there were other people in here with us." It takes a little while for Josh's heartbeat to return to normal.

"Yeah. That had me for a minute too. What do you think, time to go?"

"Definitely!"

The guys leave what they later refer to as the best scene in the maze on the only path out. They notice the path is very narrow, much narrower than most of the others they'd walked that night, but like a small capillary, it feeds into larger and larger ones, and soon they are on one of the main arteries again. Since both phones are dead and they have no flashlights, they have no way to know which way to go, and they arbitrarily turn right.

\* \* \*

"Hey, wait a minute, look here!" Julia points to a female scarecrow in a jet-black wig wearing a Pi Phi hoodie. "Do you see what I see?" In the past hour or so together and alone, Tara had been working her magic on her friend, and without Julia realizing it, she'd become her formerly cheerful self. As they finger the soft fabric of a sister's hoodie, they wonder, *Who in the world would leave their Pi Phi hoodie out here?*

Suddenly Julia looks up and puts her finger to her mouth to silence Tara. In the quiet they created, they can hear slow, deliberate footsteps crunching through the corn, somewhere not far. For a person in the middle of a cornfield with no points of reference, it's often difficult to identify the direction of a sound. In this case, however, there is no question it is getting louder and closer. But there are no voices to go along with the walking. Tara and Julia read each other's minds: *Normal people would be talking, wouldn't they?* Now the walking stops again, and they're honestly a little scared. They hold on to each other for an impossibly long time, waiting for something to happen or someone to reveal themselves. The two minutes they stand together seems like an eternity.

The rustling starts up again, louder and more noisily than before. Two creepy voices starts laughing behind them, and one seems uncomfortably close. They are still hugging, and Tara suggests in a whisper that they turn around to see where the noise is coming from. Julia nods in agreement. They execute the turn slowly, but it's an unpracticed dance, and when Julia steps on Tara's foot, she flinches and loses her balance. *Crunch.* "Shit!" Tara whispers a little too loudly. "Do you think they heard us?"

Julia feels something brushing against her left ear, but a hand against her arm prevents her from swatting at it. Simultaneously two soft fingers walk up the backs of her bare neck. "Yer mine, he-he!" rasps the assailant. When the women scream, their intruder withdraws his fingers and makes another creepy laugh. When they open their eyes and recognize the Clown from the hayride, they scream even louder and take off toward the path out of the circle.

"Wait! Don't go, it's just me," the Clown says in his normal human voice. With one smooth motion, he yanks off his latex mask and reveals his secret identity as Lucas, the guy who took their luggage earlier. "Hope I didn't scare you ladies too much."

"You scared the shit out of us!" Tara shouted, and then they burst into the kind of cathartic laughter that often comes when fear gets replaced by the familiar.

"Well, course I wanted to scare you a little."

It takes a couple minutes to catch her breath, but as soon as she can, Tara throws him a compliment. "I've got to say you guys really had us on the hayride and just now too. You were scary as hell. It was awesome, but I'm glad to know it was you."

"Yeah, well, scarin' people is a whole lot more fun than doin' chores. Ma says it's time to shut the maze down for the night 'cause a thunderstorm is on its way. She sez you got time for one last drink with everybody at the bonfire. I'm s'pposed to lead you outta here."

"Good idea. I'd hate for people to read, 'Julia Peele, struck by lightning in a corn maze. She was a sweaty hot mess when they found her.'" Lucas chuckles along with Tara.

He leads them out of the circle and in a direction they never would have thought to take. "Thunderstorm or not, I'm glad you're with us. We've gotten so turned around in here it would have taken forever to get out on our own." Julia is in a good mood.

"I know, some folks end up stayin' in here forever. Seems like we're havin' to haul somebody outta here all the time, ha-ha."

"Alive, I hope." Tara then points to Julia and back to include herself. "Is this what you call hauling out people?"

"Oh no, ma'am. This is *escortin'*. *Haulin' out's* different, ha-ha."

Lucas walks briskly, and while Julia and Tara have no trouble keeping up, they follow several paces behind him. Tara whispers to Julia, "I didn't remember he was so hot, did you? Maybe that was *his* jersey on that scarecrow?"

"Hey, Lucas. Are you by any chance a Sigma Chi?"

"Sigma what?"

"Never mind," Tara adds, with an intonation suggesting the case about Lucas and college is closed. "You kind of looked like—oh, I don't know. We guessed maybe you might be a college guy." Julia needs to shout ahead of them to be heard. "And we saw all the college sweatshirts on the scarecrows in there, and we just thought maybe you . . ."

"College? Me? Ha-ha." They're still marching in a line behind Lucas through winding and confusing paths. "Hey, Lucas. We want to come back here tomorrow, but how will we ever find this spot again? Do you have a map or something?"

"Nah, no maps. I'm the only one who really knows how this works."

"Hey, I almost forgot about Dillon and Josh. Can you help us find them?" Tara remembers. "They ditched us a long time ago and took off on their own, so they're probably lost by now, the shits. They were pretty toasted from all that cider."

Their escort laughs his hayride laugh. "He-he. Oh yeah. They's on their way out already. We've been watchin' 'em the whole time. Ma always wants everyone to be safe, you know. 'Keep all our guests safe,' she always says. 'Safety first.' He-he."

Tara grins. "Your laugh is just too creepy."

# 13

It seemed a little roundabout at first, but Lucas explained he was taking them the scenic way back. Even so, it only took about ten minutes to get to where they could see the exit ahead and Josh and Dillon waiting for them.

"Hey, thanks again for doing this. You really know your way around here."

"I should, I made it," Lucas replies modestly. "I make it every year. If I have to, I can get out of anywhere in the maze in three and a half minutes, he-he."

"Would you be willing to give us a private tour?" Julia elbows Tara to suggest she's not going to be a part of that.

"Whenever you want to, ma'am." He has to look over his shoulder and shout to converse with them, because he's walking so much faster than they are. When they emerge from the exit, Josh is the first to greet them. "Hey, word is everyone's meeting back at the bonfire for one more drink."

"I don't know. I'm really tired. Think I'll just go up to the room and hit the sack," she said. "Want to come with me?"

"Sorry, ma'am," Lucas interrupts, "but Ma likes to make sure everyone is out of the maze before closing up for the night. It'll only take a few minutes."

"Safety first, right?" Tara mimics and flirts at the same time.

All five wander across the field to the growing crowd of people already drinking and carrying on. Ma is there, and Lucy's playing waitress with her jug of cider. Both guys head over to her right away; Josh feigns a great thirst he's developed navigating the maze, and Dillon insists he requires cider for medicinal purposes.

"OK," Ma announces. "Looks like we're all here, but I want to count noses to be sure. Let's see—one, two, three. Who's over there? Oh, I see. Four, five . . ."

"Here's Travis, y'all!" Tara follows the voice to Shelly, the girlfriend of the guy who got pulled off the wagon and whose head they last saw the Clown bashing against the hay wagon. Shelly is pointing to the skinny guy at her side. The crowd breaks into unrehearsed applause and someone shouts, "Glad you got him back." Shelly is grinning ear to ear, and she holds up Travis's hand for all to see. "You and me both!" Someone else yells, "He's got quite a head on his shoulders!" and the crowd groans from the bad joke.

"Okay. All present and accounted for." Ma has finished doing her safety check. "Now *bottoms up*, everybody, and then head back to the house. Storm's not gonna wait much longer."

"What about Carrie?" Julia asks Ma.

"Oh, *her*. I counted her already. She wasn't feeling up to snuff. The night must've did her in, I reckon."

*How come I had to be here in person and she didn't?* Julia is a bit perturbed.

"I'd feel better if I saw her," Julia counters. "I think I'll go pay a visit to her room."

"Oh, sweet thing. I wouldn't think she'd want you to see her tonight. That one, she's a real mess, gittin' dragged all over tarnation 'n' the rest. I seen her." Ma giggles a bit. "What a picture!"

"Speaking of pictures, Dillon and I saw the dummy of her in the maze, polka-dot scarf and all. Oh, yeah. Carrie was in on it all right. We took a selfie with her 'dead body.'" Josh uses air quotes. "I'd show you now, but my phone's dead. It was pretty cool."

"Sounds like a couple a somebodies didn't stay on the path!" Ma chides with a smile.

"Yeah, sorry about that. But it was pretty cool, except for getting paint on our jeans."

Ma stoops down to look. "I'm sorry about that, young man. You jest drop them pants off in the morning. I got sumthin' that'll get that stain right out."

"Still, I'd rather see her actual body, not some dummy," Julia protests.

"Oh, she's no dummy. I'll give her that," sniffs Ma, and she turns to leave for the house.

"C'mon, Jules. Just admit it. They put on a really good show, and you enjoyed it," whines Josh.

"Well, we had fun too, no thanks to you two ditching us right away. Jules and I found this spot where there's a bunch of college student scarecrows wearing jerseys and sweatshirts," said Tara. "Georgetown was represented, you'll be please to know."

"Honey, I think it's time to take you back to the room. You're toasted," Julia says to her husband. Josh is disappointed she's nagging at him, but he's encouraged by being called *honey* and by the shift in his wife's attitude.

There's a bit of a shift in the wind too and, not too far off, a flash and the rumble of thunder. "It's late, Josh." He doesn't look her way.

"I don't think I'm ready to turn in yet. I need to wind down some first," Dillon offers.

"Me too," Josh says with a wink.

"Okay by me," Tara pipes in.

"Well, okay then!" Dillon sounds more enthusiastic now.

"How about you, Jules?"

"Well, why not, if everyone else is staying up."

# 14

"**S**uite Number 7," as it turns out, is the smallest guest room in the house by any measurement. The ceilings are low and sloped, and Josh has to bend his neck even to stand, so from his forty-five-degree angle, the room looks even smaller. Not that he can stand up. One drink led to another, and the partying friends finally called it quits a little past two. As inebriated as he is, though, Josh shares the same horrified expression as his wife. *Are you kidding me?*

The focal point of the suite is a twin bed that would fit maybe two small children uncomfortably, and their Louis Vuitton luggage takes up the remaining floor space, except for the child-sized dresser against one wall.

"I thought Ma said we had a suite?"

"She did. I heard her too. I'm sure there must be some mistake."

"Probably that dumb Lucy got mixed it up. If Tara had let me come to our room when we first arrived, I could have said something. So what are you going to do about it? I can't sleep here."

"Well, it's after two, and we can't wake Ma up now. I'll get it straightened out in the morning, promise." Josh's head is spinning.

"Yeah, and I want our money back too. This is ridiculous!" It hasn't taken Julia long for her mood to swing.

*Crack! Boom!* Thunder and lightning add to the drama of the evening, and renegade tree branches bang against the windows for good measure. Josh mutters something incomprehensible as the wild thunderstorm struts its stuff right outside their window. The eaves can't handle the volume, and extra bursts of water splash and smack against the siding. Josh has already forgotten where he is, and when the last bolt of lightning releases its thunderclap, he bumps his head on the ceiling. In a daze, he pulls off all his clothes and leaves them in a pile on the floor. He collapses spread-eagle in a stupor on the bed.

"Okay," she says in a full voice, pretending he'll be interested. "I'm just gonna go find the bathroom. I'll be right back." She can hear him snoring even before she finishes speaking.

The large bathroom is off the upstairs hallway, just across the hall and down a bit from their room. *Why is our bathroom down the hall? Some suite.* Julia stares at herself in the mirror above the sink for a long time and then turns on the water. It is one of those old-fashioned faucets with the porcelain cross handles. *Elizabethan,* she remembers from a photo shoot she once styled. She just loves how it fits her hand. They had been all the rage for a while before the trends swung around one hundred and eighty degrees to ultra modern. Still, you have to pay a pretty penny for these online now. A quick survey around to the combination tub and shower confirms all the faucets are that style. Nice. On second glance, almost all. The handle to switch the water from the faucet to the showerhead is a generic one from Home Depot or somewhere and doesn't fit in. But the overall loveliness of the bathroom temporarily defuses some of her anger and disappointment over their bedroom.

She fishes around in her purse for a prescription bottle and taps a pill onto her palm. She stares at it for a moment and then taps out two more. The familiar woman who is glaring at her from inside the mirror is cautioning her not to take them on top of all the alcohol she had in her system, but the stern warning doesn't deter her. She cups her hands to take a gulp or two of water to help swallow them, and with her hands still cupped, she splashes cold water over her face and turns off the water. She doesn't bother to dry her face but merely stands motionless, listening to the howling wind and thinking about Carrie, of all things.

*Whack!* A tree branch smacks hard against the window. It is loud enough and surprising enough to give her a jolt, and she lets out a tiny scream. A long lightning flash silhouettes that same large branch that startled her, and another long rumble follows it.

She stares at the drain in the bottom of the sink for more time than she needs to compose herself because looking into the mirror reminds her how horrible she looks. But something just outside the bathroom makes her eyes shift to the door she hasn't quite closed all the way. *Stupid me. Why did I leave the door open?* She is reaching to pull it shut when *bang*—someone else slams it shut for her, and that person is now scrambling away down the hallway.

Julia opens the door a crack and peeks out. "Hello?" It takes a few moments for her eyes to adjust to the darkness again, but she thinks she sees a slight shadow cast against the wall by a faint light source down the hall and around the corner. She hasn't remembered seeing any pets in the house. "Hello?" she asks again, a little louder but still tentatively. Silence. Whatever she thinks might be there isn't moving until she takes one stealth step forward and it scurries away loudly down the back stairway. It sounds to her like it has two feet, not four, so she decides what she saw was a who and not a what. When it bolts, it gives her such a start she falls backward against the door, and when it swings open wide, she falls through the doorway and onto the black-and-white tiled floor. The doorknob bangs loudly against the tiled walls. "Good grief!" Outside in the hall, all is calm, but outside the house, the storm continues to rage, and the night is anything but silent.

# 15

She has an idea and checks her watch. Two thirty. She guessed the tiny bit of light she saw coming from around the corner a few minutes ago might be enough to find the room with the wreath on its door, and she tiptoes down the hall to look for it. The sleeping pills haven't had time to do their job, and she is still wide awake. She has plenty of time for this mission, since she is in no particular rush to share that impossibly small bed with Josh. She leans against the door frame of Carrie's room and whispers, "Carrie? Carrie? It's me, Julia."

From behind, a strong hand lands firmly on her shoulder. She screeches and whips around to see the hand belongs to Dillon, who is standing in his pajamas with a toothbrush still in his mouth.

"Whoa, sorry! You scared me. I heard screaming and doors slamming."

"I scared you? *You* scared me."

Silence.

"You OK?"

"I don't know."

"What do you mean you don't know? So what are you doing out here in the hall?"

"I think someone was snooping on me."

"For Pete's sake, Jules. Look who's doing the snooping."

She jiggles the knob to open Carrie's door. "She knows something, and I want to know what."

"Since when do you think barging into a stranger's room in the middle of the night is OK? Besides, I thought we all agreed she was in on the whole scary hayride bit. What are you worried about?"

"But we didn't see her at the end, when were all were drinking around the bonfire. Don't you think it's a little strange the other guy who got abducted was there and she wasn't?"

"No. Not at all. I really never thought about it, though. Maybe she went to bed. Maybe she doesn't drink. Maybe it's because they cut her head off, ha-ha." Then he becomes more frank. "Seriously, Jules, I have to be honest with you. This obsession with Carrie is getting a little boring."

"I don't care if you're bored. I know it looked like she was in on it and everything, but I swear there was just something about her. Call it a woman's intuition."

"How about we call it *acting*? Anyway I think Ma said it best—'She's a bit *off*.'"

"Yeah, that's what Ma wanted us to believe." Julia elbows past him to knock on the door again, but he stops it by grabbing her hand.

"Oh god, now *you're* sounding like Carrie."

"She told me to meet her in her room tonight. She said she was afraid for her life and that if she didn't meet us tonight to call the police."

"I thought she wanted to meet in the morning? Remember? Some stupid time, like seven thirty."

"On the hayride she told me things had gotten more serious and that I absolutely had to see her tonight. She made me promise."

"*Things* got worse? What things? How?"

"I don't know exactly, but when she was talking about the woman getting murdered yesterday, I think she meant Shelly. Don't forget she pointed at me and yelled out her name as that creep carried her off the wagon. And she gave that other scream at the end of the hayride too. Her last word was *Shelly*."

"That's because she wasn't pointing at you. She was pointing to an actual Shelly, the guy's girlfriend sitting right next to you. Christ, Julia, listen to yourself. It doesn't make sense."

"She was telling me she remembered Shelly's name."

"Ma already told us Shelly never got here. And anyway, who thinks Shelly is dead besides Carrie? Nobody. And why would they? Why are you working so hard at making this a thing?"

"Well, of course, if Ma killed her, she'd say that, wouldn't she? Besides, a woman on the hayride verified a woman with a baby was here yesterday. Didn't you hear her?"

"I heard what she said, Julia. She didn't verify anything. She said there was *a* woman with *a* baby at the farm yesterday. There must have been tons. The place was crawling with families and kids."

"Well, okay. That's true."

"For pete's sake, why would Ma want to kill her anyway? I thought you watched television. What's her motive? C'mon," he says, reaching out for a hug, "it's late, and we've all had a fair amount to drink. Give it a rest. I think someone needs to go beddy-bye."

He takes her hand and leads her back to her bedroom.

# 16

She could have heard him snoring outside their room even if the door wasn't ajar, but she makes a mental note to close all the doors securely from now on. Just in case she might wake him, Julia moves quietly and pushes the door open silently anyway. The light that was on in their room abruptly goes off. *What the ... ?* She tries the wall switch just inside the door. Nothing. She gropes ahead in the dark for the cut-glass lamp she remembered seeing on the room's small dresser and, turning it on, reveals Lucy in a floor-length nightgown standing at the foot of the bed. She is holding a jug of cider in one hand and a flashlight in the other. She had obviously been staring at Josh, who was sleeping naked and exposed with the blankets pulled down, and she knew she'd been caught in the act.

"What are *you* doing here with my husband?"

Lucy hands the jug to Julia and makes a curtsy, like an upstairs maid in a BBC production might do on her way out. "Beggin' yer pardon. Ma asked me to bring Josh his cider."

"Bring *Josh* his cider? Kind of late for room service, don't you think?" Julia is a little heated. She storms over to Josh's bed and hurriedly throws a blanket over him to cover him up.

"Were you the one in the hall too?" she demands. "Earlier?"

Lucy doesn't say anything else, but she lowers her head, stares at the floor, and scurries out of the room, her exit punctuated by a very loud thunderclap. When she disappears around the corner, Julia closes the door to their room and stands silently for a moment before cracking up. She decides to dismiss Lucy as a "boy-crazy" nitwit and finds the whole incident pretty funny.

Right now, though, she's dead tired, and she needs to figure out how to fit into the inadequate little bed Josh hadn't taken long to monopolize.

She cocoons herself into a little space she manages to create, but no matter how much she struggles to find even the slightest semblance of comfort, she fails. She stares at the ceiling in frustration for a moment before getting up, grabbing one of the blankets and a pillow, and heading out the door. *There has to be a sofa around here somewhere.*

* * *

It is pitch black in the house, and the storm is in full force. Julia has only taken one step down the stairs before she pauses. *What the hell, it'll only take a second.* Moments later, she is back at Carrie's bedroom door, ready to knock. She doesn't want to tap too hard because she doesn't want Dillon to hear, but she's not sure she really wants it to be loud enough for Carrie to hear either.

What she is about to do reminds her of one of her lazy bosses. He would wait to return phone calls from people he didn't want to talk to until he was sure they had left for their day. He'd boast that he could always say he'd called but that they weren't there. Then he could put them off a little more by moving their call slip to the bottom of his stack. That would have been during the age of landlines, of course, when people had to leave their phones behind them when they walked out of their offices. But Julia considers she is essentially doing the same thing now. Could knocking so faintly that Carrie couldn't possibly hear be enough to say she tried to fulfill her promise? *I knocked, but nobody answered.* She drops her arm to her side; she is in no shape to have this moral debate right now. Besides, she wonders how much she is really invested in Carrie's theories.

In the end, she leaves without knocking and returns to the front of the house. As she takes her first step down the long stairway, bold flashes of lightning dazzle dramatically through the rain-splotched window on the landing. It makes for quite a picture, and she snickers to think of the crazy night they were all spending in this creaky old house, complete with a thunderstorm, the innkeeper's nutty daughter, and a crazy lady down the hall.

Because the house is so dark inside and she is so unfamiliar with her surroundings, she is grateful for those occasional lightning bolts, which for fleeting moments illuminate the next section of staircase in front of her. Once in the front foyer, she turns to follow the long main hallway that leads to the rear of the house. It zigzags to conform to all the additions to the house, and she has to grope her way along the hallway with her hands, inch by inch. *Wall, wall, wall—what the . . . ? What's this?* She stumbles a bit as she sidesteps around one of those antique hall trees she doesn't remember seeing before and is thankful she didn't knock it over. *OK, back to the wall. Wall, wall, doorframe.* As she feels her way across this next feature, she can feel a cool stream of air from inside the door. It smells damp and dank, and she scrunches her nose a little, guessing it's the door to the basement. She silently vows not to go down there on a bet, and she's just about to continue past it, when she thinks she hears something.

The clatter of the storm is vying for her attention with whatever the sound coming from below might be, and it is difficult to tell what she hears. She turns the doorknob, but another latch is preventing it from opening. She feels up and down the frame to find it, when her hand passes over a sliding bolt. She pinches the little knob with her thumb and index finger and tugs it down to slide it open. *Clack.* A strong blast of unpleasant air smacks her in the face, when the bolt is released and the door pops open.

For a second it occurs to her she is probably trespassing or, at the very least, doing something she shouldn't be doing. To be certain she is as quiet as possible, she pulls it open slowly, only a few centimeters at a time. *So far, so good.* The next centimeter doesn't come without a fight, though. *Squeak!* It is impossible the noise can be so loud and so drawn out, and it almost makes her laugh out loud. *Crap! I hope nobody heard that.* She waits a few minutes before she continues. There is still silence in the house. *Whew!* Now the hinges are cooperating, and it is almost wide enough for her to stick her head in. *Screech!* The noise is louder and more piercing this time, like an alarm. *When was the last time anyone oiled these hinges?* The moment is tense and absurd and creepy and laughable at the same time. *Bam!* A door slams shut somewhere in another part of the house. *I've only got a few seconds.*

Even in the dark, with her head poked into the landing, she can make out the crude, steep stairway leading down to the old cellar. "Hello. Anybody down there?" The response is a frantic crashing and banging commotion, as though someone in a hurry has just knocked over some boxes or furniture. She thinks she hears a very tired voice pleading, "Help me."

Julia froze. "Who's down there?" *Clank! Clank! Clank!* Somewhere in the darkness, the ancient furnace fires up, and it groans and whirrs like something from another century, which of course it is. It catches her completely by surprise, and she jumps backward out of the doorway and bangs up against the wall behind her, knocking one of the framed photographs off the wall. The glass shatters when it clatters to the floor. *More noise.* Now she has no time to lose. She has to find a sofa fast, and if anyone comes by, she can always pretend she has been asleep and play dumb.

Embarrassed and frightened, Julia tiptoes down the hall and zips into the small parlor she remembers having seen. She fumbled to find the light switch. *Click. Click, click. Don't any of the light switches work in this house?* This room is every bit as dark as the rest of the house, but illumination streaming through the window from a small floodlight on an outbuilding is enough for her to look around, and there against a wall is the sofa she needs. With one swift motion, she flings down her pillow, plops down, and covers herself perfectly and evenly with the blanket. If anyone wandered in at that moment, they would probably have burst out laughing. Lying there stiffly under the perfectly smooth blanket, Julia is as convincing as a nine-year-old pretending to be asleep past her bedtime. She waits and waits.

It has been several minutes, and nobody has come. *My god, Julia, come to your senses!* With her head on a pillow, she has finally begun to relax, and she now she's wondering what in the world made her think there had been voices coming from the basement. The house was full of odd sounds. *All that worrying for nothing.* She's safe now and can rest. Just in case, though, she decides to wait another few minutes before opening her eyes.

When she does open them, she's stunned to find the small parlor lined on three sides with shelves all crammed with dolls. There must be a couple of hundred. *Good grief!* There are boy dolls and girl dolls, she guesses, but since the faces painted on the burlap heads are all identical and all the clothes are made from the same fabric, she can't tell. Just across from the sofa is another smaller display of similar dolls, but this time piled precariously in a stack like a pyramid. The creepy doll on top is staring directly at Julia through the empty eyeholes torn through its sack, and now that she knows it's looking at her, she won't be able to sleep unless she can figure out a way to cover it. She stands up and snatches the afghan from the back of the sofa and carefully draped it over the pile. *Perfect.* There is one more doll, though, the afghan wasn't long enough to hide, and it stares at her from the bottom of the pile. *Yech!* She grabs a throw pillow from the sofa and arranges it in to block her view. *Success!*

As she backs up to admire her work, she bumps into Ma, who has somehow entered the room without her noticing. "Where did you come from?" she gasps. She spins around and catches the corner of the afghan with one of her feet, toppling the whole display. "Oh my gosh. I'm so sorry!"

"Oh no, dearie. I'm the one who's sorry. I didn't mean to frighten ya," Ma apologizes. "I heard some noise and wuz afraid something just wasn't right." She reaches out to hold Julia, who is doing her best to compose herself.

"It's all right. Our bed was so small I thought I'd try sleeping on the sofa in here. I'm fine, but I ruined your doll display. Here, let me just put them back together, and then I'll just go back upstairs." Julia avoids looking Ma in the eye because she is embarrassed, but she is glad at least she hadn't been caught snooping around the basement door.

"Dearie, wait. Leave that." Julia stops what she was doing. She is a wreck. "I know you ain't fine. Would it be all right if I called you Julia?"

"Huh? Oh, sure."

"I've been around long enough to know when a couple's in trouble, now haven't I?" Julia is not certain Ma is looking for a response. She's humiliated, and after having been scared silly several times tonight, she's not in the mood for an interrogation about her marriage by a stranger. "I seen it wuz bad when you came in, but seein' you two ain't sleepin' in the same bed—well, that's awful worrisome."

"I appreciate you are trying to help, but I really need to get to bed."

Ma cuts her off. "Please. Let me get you some hot cocoa." Ma turns on a little floor lamp, which barely adds any light to the room.

"Ma'am, I don't need anything to drink. I just need—"

"Come on into the kitchen, now. I insist," Ma presses on. "And call me Ma, everybody does."

The storm is still thrashing. Julia remembers the comfort Ma gave her after that traumatic hayride and gives in, but she can't help glancing back at the dolls before she follows Ma down the back hall and into the kitchen. *Weird.*

"Oh, I see you like my doll collection." Ma smiles. "Made 'em all myself, an' when you've got some time, I'll show 'em to you proper. Now take a seat at the table if you like, dearie, an' I'll bring over the cocoa."

"Yes, by all means, please call me Julia." She has decided she'd prefer to be on a first name basis rather than dearie, which sounds like a name the witch might have called Hansel or Gretel.

"I know'd Pa my whole life, and everyone in the family always said they know'd he wuz the one for me." The old metal coffee pot she used for making hot chocolate was already rattling on one of the stove's burners, a sign she had started making it earlier. Apparently Ma hadn't slept very well either.

"But—well, let's just say there's been trying times." She grabs two mugs from the cupboard and sets them in front of Julia. "You'll always question yerself, Julia. Ya cain't help it. An' when it gets to be more work than fun and games, ya start questioning even more. But when it comes down to it, it's about needs. If you can give each other what you need, then everything will be okay. If you cain't, well then, you best find somebody who can."

Ma poured the steaming cocoa into Julia's mug and then reached for the jug with a big *W* written on it. It surprised Julia to see Ma yank its cork out with her teeth the way Lucy had, but it looked just as idiotic. *Like mother, like daughter*, she guessed.

"Been a long day for me, an' I need a little something stronger. Go ahead, Julia. Don't be shy. Drink up. This is gonna help you sleep." The cocoa is delicious, and after the first sip, Julia needs no further encouragement.

"What's in it?" She takes another long drink.

"Oh, snips an' snails and puppy dog tails," Ma jokes. "Say, that's an awfully purty necklace yer wearin'. I noticed it right off when you got here."

The cocoa doesn't take long to loosen her up, and soon Julia finds herself uncharacteristically chatty. "Thanks. It was a gift from Josh's mom. I don't care much for her, but I love the necklace. It's an old piece from Tiffany."

"You got a relative named Tiffany, too? Land sakes. Well, it's real purty."

"You know, I hate to admit it, but the reason I asked you what was in the cocoa was because I had just taken a couple of sleeping pills, and I didn't want to drink anything that would give me a bad reaction. My doctor recently put me on antidepressants too, and I'm not supposed to drink alcohol. That's why I didn't want to drink any of your cider. But I ended up drinking a little because Josh doesn't know I take them." She hardly stops between sentences.

"Oh, you poor sweet thing. If you want, I got another room you can bunk in fer tonight. Since yer friend didn't show up, you can sleep in hers."

"Oh no. It's awfully thoughtful of you, but I just couldn't." Not so deep down, she thinks a nice comfortable room might really be just what the doctor might order if he were here, and she hopes Ma would make the offer again.

Ma twinkles, "Better there than on that lumpy ol' davenport you wuz plannin' on sleepin' on. You need a proper rest, Julia––a long winter's rest."

Now she was feeling a little loopy. "Okay, Ma," she responded, downing the remaining concoction in one big gulp. "So where's that bedroom?"

# 17

Ma's key ring is big and round, like the ones sheriffs use in westerns to unlock their jail cells. There are enough keys to fill half the ring, but her fingers go straight to the right one she needs. The door opens to a long, spacious, and somehow tastefully decorated bedroom, and Julia is thrilled to see the private bath off the other end. *Now this is a suite.*

"Welcome to your new home, Julia."

Julia drags herself in, struggling to keep her eyes open. She lets loose a cavernous yawn. "It's warm in here."

Ma smiles. "It is, indeed, but it's probably my cocoa talkin' to ya. It's my great Meemaw Minnie's special recipe, and it'll warm you down to the bone."

"But what about . . ." Julia loses her train of thought as Ma pulls back the covers on the bed.

"What about what?" Ma asks.

"What about that person in your basement?" Julia mumbles.

"You been down in our cellar? Now ain't that something." Ma is all smiles.

"No, of course not, but I'm pretty sure I heard someone down there crying for help."

"Land sakes alive, girl! We've got eleven or twelve bedrooms here and more in the back, so Ma 'n' Pa sure 'nuff don't need to put folks up down in the cellar now, do we?" She chuckles. "An' screamin' for help, good glory!"

"And then I think the furnace must have gone on and I—"

"You know, every time that ol' furnace kicks on, Pa an' me is grateful. Don't want to have to put in a new one, so we don't mind when it talks to us. There's lots of noises in this ol' house now, sweetie, an' with the storm an' all."

"And Lucy was spying on Josh. And—"

"Listen to you now. Somebody did this, and they did that. People yellin' in the cellar, Peepin' Toms running wild. I declare, you'd think we wuz in *New York city.*"

"And Carrie said you murdered my friend Shelly." She's feeling a lot more docile and less inhibited, but enunciating is more difficult, and her eyelids are heavy. "She told me not to trust you, but she must have been wrong. I can trust you, Ma, can't I?"

At the mention of Carrie, Ma's tone becomes frosty. "That Masterson woman was poking her nose where it didn't belong."

Julia is still sitting on the edge of the bed, struggling to stay awake. "She told me to call the police if something happened to her. And she's not in her room, I checked." Julia drags out her last observation.

"Okay now, I'm gonna let you go to sleep. Sweet dreams, purty girl."

"Okay."

Ma goes out into the hall and shuts the door behind her. Now it's her turn to roll her eyes and shake her head.

In spite of her diminished faculties, she remembers her door needs to be locked. It takes a moment to force herself to stand up, but she manages to stagger over to the door to flip the lever of the big blocky iron door lock. *Clank!* Then she turns off the lights. She's still fully clothed when she collapses onto her new soft and very spacious featherbed. Only light rain is falling outside her window now, and her cares have all melted away. She closes her eyes. *Much better.*

* * *

It's still pitch black and quiet in her room. At first it sounds unspecific, like any of the sounds the might come from the general shifting and creaking of an old frame house. With so many chemical influences controlling different bits of her brain, it is remarkable any sound at all penetrates her foggy state, but somehow she detects a noise in the room. "Who's there?" Her voice is feeble but apparently loud enough to cause whatever was making the sound to stop.

The silence induces sobriety for only a split second, but when the drugs takes over again, she convinces herself it was probably just the pipes, like Ma had suggested, or the wind, or something else. And her eyes are just too heavy, and frankly she just doesn't care. Her whole body slackens and falls quiet. In a few moments, something makes the floorboards creak again.

She struggles to interpret the noises, but since her mind isn't working very well, she decides to try her eyes. She flails one of her arms toward the lamp on the bedside table, but her movements are imprecise, and she only manages to knock it over. Meemaw's antique lamp rolls along the top of the table and off the side, but its short electrical cord catches it from falling to the floor. Instead it dangles off the edge, swinging like a pendulum, and the cut-glass globe shatters when it smashes against one of the table legs. Julia falls unconscious. *Out like a light.*

# 18

osh wakes up alone and confused. *Where's Julia? Did she already go to breakfast without me?* Sometimes at home she'd sleep in another room if he was snoring a lot, but he wonders how she could have done that here. Grumpy and a little hung over, he heaves himself out of bed, and with one hand against his pounding head and the other holding up the towel around his waist, he staggers out into the hall, in search of his bathroom.

The tub and shower are old and huge, and there is plenty of water pressure to wake him up. He closes his eyes and allows the therapeutic steam to swirl around him. *Ah.* He's in the zone, thinking about how fun it was last night and acknowledging he just can't drink like he used to. Suddenly the lights in the bathroom go out. The transparent shower curtain has become translucent from the steam, and he can't see anything, so he pokes his head around the curtain. "Somebody there?" Hearing no reply, he tries a different approach. "Hey! Hello, I'm taking a shower. Hey, turn the light back on, please."

He's covered with soapsuds, but he decides he can rinse off later. This is an emergency. He turns off the water and slides back the shower curtain. The side of the tub is unusually tall, and when he lifts one leg high over the edge to step out, the full weight of his body teeters unstably on the leg standing on the slippery bottom of the tub. He lets out an *uh-oh*, and as he slips, he grabs the shower curtain for support, and both curtain and rod come crashing down on top of him. "What the . . . ?" It's so steamy in the room he can hardly see to extricate himself from the rod and the wet, soapy shower curtain.

Josh figures his intruder will be long gone if he waits to untangle himself from all the pieces of the wet mess, so he decides to wrap the shower curtain around his waist and waddle to the door. "Polka Dots, that you?" He sticks his head out the door and surveys the hallway. *Nothing.* "Just so you know, I'm on to you!" he shouts, half in jest. There is still no response. Frustrated, he goes back into the dark bathroom and slams the door shut. The light flickers back on. "Huh?" Looking at the broken curtain rod on the floor and the trail of shower curtain behind him, he concludes his day isn't starting out well. *Now how the hell am I going to put this all back together so I can finish my shower?*

# 19

Dillon and Tara are just finishing up another of their animated conversations, where they laugh and use their hands a lot. They're seated at one end of the long rustic table in the Winters' pretty dining room, when Josh shuffles into the room and plops down next to Dillon. His hair is still damp.

"How did you sleep?" Dillon asks him. "Tara and I were out like lights."

"Night was fine. The morning was a little weird though. Hey, how do I get coffee? You seen Jules?"

Dillon and Tara share a concerned look. "I don't know. I thought she'd be with you. Is she even up yet?" The door to the kitchen swings open, and Ma bursts in as if on cue with a pot of coffee and a cup for Josh.

"Couldn't help overhearing what y'all wuz saying. I put yer wife up in the room yer friend wuz going to use," Ma informs them. "Seems she couldn't sleep or sumthin' like that." Ma sets a bottle of aspirin on the table in front of Josh before returning to her kitchen.

Josh holds his aching head with both hands, digesting this new information from Ma. "Hey thanks for the aspirin." Then he turns to the others. "How did she know I . . . ?"

Dillon and Tara lift the hands up together to mime the "I don't know, she seems to know everything" look.

"Wonderful. It's nice to know we're sleeping in separate beds now. That's good for a relationship, right?" he adds sarcastically.

An awkward silence engulfs the room until Ma sticks her head through the door again. "Pa says he heard some crashing around upstairs a little while ago. Wuz everything all right?"

"Yeah, sorry about that. Someone came in and turned off the bathroom lights when I was taking a shower! Kind of freaked me out."

"Really?" Dillon quizzes. "Who would do that?"

"I dunno. I was about to check when the effing shower curtain fell down on top of me, and by the time I got over to the door, they were gone."

"Ha-ha," Tara jokes. "*They* were gone? Now the *someone* is a *they*?"

"I couldn't actually see who it was, but I mean it had to be someone. I was in the shower when the lights went off, and doors don't just open and close by themselves."

Ma walks in again with a basket of biscuits for Josh. "Well they sure 'nuff do here, young man. This old house is full of creaking and drafts and such. Doors blow open and shut all the time. I swear it drives Pa crazy. Yer wife thought she heard noises too last night, poor dear. Voices callin' out, all kinds of things. Ha-ha. We both had a good laugh about that last night. I declare, you city folk. Oh, an' Pa wuz messin' with the fuses this morning a little while ago. 'Bout that time, I reckon. Might a been him."

Ma retreats back to the kitchen again. "Hope you like yer eggs fried. Oh, and did I mention you share that bathroom with the folks in Room 9, so maybe . . ."

"Wait! What? We have a suite, and we share that bathroom? Huh? And you and she were up talking last night? This is all too much."

Ma continues the conversation through the closed door. "Yeah, we had a little girl talk back in there 'round my kitchen table 'til I don't know how late. She's a fine one, that wife of yers, purty too."

"While we're on the subject, Ma, I've got to talk to you today about getting switched to a different room. Hope you don't mind."

"Oh, I'm way ahead of ya. There must have been some kind of mix-up. We'll get it straightened out today."

"That extra room reminds me. Shelley still hasn't shown up. I'm gonna text her right now." Tara rummages around in her bag for her cell phone.

Josh begins to fiddle with his phone too. "Anyone have service?" Dillon checks his.

"I could've sworn I had a couple bars earlier," Tara says.

"I have data," Dillon waves his phone proudly.

"You do?" Josh asks.

"Wait, I lied." He gives in to the inevitable and places his phone on the table. "It's gone. Wait! What's this network—0824641611? Says it needs a password."

Ma enters the dining room with Lucas, who's carrying fresh juice in a vintage glass pitcher straight out of a Kool-Aid commercial. He sets it down in front of Josh and returns to the kitchen.

"Who's the dude?" Josh asks Dillon in a half whisper.

Dillon is stunned by the extent of Josh's cluelessness. "He took your luggage up to your room yesterday."

Pointing toward the kitchen, Tara mouths, "And he was the Clown."

"Hey! Can you give us the password to your Wi-Fi?" Josh asks loud enough for anyone and nobody in particular to hear.

Walking back through the door, Ma responds, "We have a hi-fi back in our livin' room, but it don't have a password. Yer hi-fi has a password?"

"Hi-fi? What's a hi-fi?" Tara asks, not looking up from her phone.

"No, the password to your Wi-Fi network."

Josh now puts his faith in Lucas and shouts toward the kitchen so he can hear him. "Seriously Lucas, you do have Wi-Fi in the house, right?"

Josh hasn't noticed Lucas is already back in the dining room. "I'm right here, and no, sir, we don't. Ma told us she heard it causes cancer."

Tara kicks Josh with her foot under the table. There's astonishment in her eyes.

"But you do have some Internet though, don't you? Please say you do."

Ma sticks her head back through the door again. "A course we do. We ain't a bunch of ol' hicks, now are we? But Lucy's the expert on all that, an' you'll have to ask her about it. I declare that young lady keeps up on everything."

Tara and Dillon share eye rolls again. "Lucy *is* tech support."

Josh turns to Lucas and moves his thumbs over his iPhone screen like he's playing a game. "Really? You don't, you know, play any . . . ?"

Lucas shakes his head.

"Lucas, I'll bet if you ask him nicely, Josh will show you how to play Pumpkin Menace."

"Oh no, don't get Lucas addicted to that game too," Tara intervenes.

"Land sakes, I don't see what all the fuss about this Innernet is anyway. Anyways, yer not gonna get it today on account of the big storm last night. The boys say the phone line's down or all fried up or sumthin'. Phone company cain't git out till Tuesday to fix it."

All three gulp and look at each other in disbelief. *Dialup? No Internet for three more days?* Two unthinkables. Which one was worse?

"You're joking, right? What about this network I'm seeing? Who does it belong to?"

"Network? Land sakes! That's probably NBC. We git that, don't we, Lucas? Is that what y'all mean? Where's Lucy when we need her? Now what else we can git you? It's gonna be a big day for everybody around here. Our last day with all these people around. Tomorrow it'll be just family. Hooray."

"Don't forget us, we'll still be here." Dillon adds.

"Glory, no. We ain't fergetting you. Pa an' Lucas an' Lucy and me, we wuz all sayin' how nice y'all is an' how much we feel yer already part of the family. Nah, I wuz talkin' about the other folks, our customers." Ma heads back to the kitchen, mumbling, "Network. Land sakes alive, now why would we have our own network?" Tara kicks Josh under the table again and shoots him a look that says, *Be nice.*

Lucas stands up and asks if anyone wants more coffee. As he heads to the kitchen, Tara gestures with her thumb at the departing Lucas and does Ma's Groucho Marx thing with her eyebrows.

"Am I crazy, or is Farm Boy kinda hot?"

"Um, yeah, Tara, you're crazy," Dillon says with a smile.

"You think anyone in pants is hot, Tara." Josh and Dillon then turn to each other and share a laugh.

"No, seriously guys. I mean, I'm out here alone for a couple of days, and you know."

"Oh, go for it, Tara. You know you're going to anyway."

"Come on. A girl's got to have a little fun, you know. Besides, I thought I caught him looking at me a few times."

"OK, Tara. Say no more. We get it," Josh comments, as though they've been there before. "But I kinda thought it was Dillon he was looking at. I mean it could have been. He's sitting right next to you."

"Not my type! Tara, he's all yours."

"You're impossible, Josh!"

"I'm just kidding, Tara. Yes, he's perfect for you. Go for it."

Tara tries to change the subject. "Hey, Ma. Those were some crazy pumpkin people we saw in your Corn Maze last night. Julia and I were in that big circle with all those school sweatshirts. What's the connection? Did you and Pa go to some fancy schools?" She can't believe how much she's patronizing her.

By now everyone assumes Ma would be listening on the other side of the swinging kitchen door, which is why Tara didn't even bother raising her voice when she asked and why it only took a second for Ma to pop her head back out again to answer. "Schools? Oh, glory no. We home school, a Winter tradition. Some of the schools out there are teachin' a lot of nonsense, you know."

"So where did you get them? Steal 'em from the guests?" Tara giggles.

"This farm's like one big ol' Lost and Found," Lucas explains. "If nobody comes back to git stuff, we just use it for sumthin'. Ma don't like to waste nuthin'."

Ma adds, shouting a little from the kitchen, "An' those scarecrows are all Lucas's babies. Sometimes I swear he'd rather dress them up than go huntin' with Pa."

Josh and Tara immediately stare at Dillon. "Why are you all looking at me?"

"Oh shit! Polka Dots!" Josh remembers their appointment.

"I forgot about her too," Tara adds.

"What did you all think was so bad about her? I forgot," Dillon asks offhandedly.

"Well, she's a clinger, that one is."

"'That one is.' When did you start talking like that, Josh?" Dillon laughs.

"I know a clinger when I see one, and this ol' bitch will stick like Krazy Glue. That other woman could see her comin' a mile away."

"Comin'? Josh. Y'all sound like you wuz born here," mimics Dillon.

"She'll play tour guide, and everything will seem just dandy. Then she'll join us for vittles at lunch, and then she'll want to have dinner with us." Josh is holding court now. "Come on, let's get out of here before she shows up and starts creeping on us again."

"Who ya talkin' about, if ya don't mind my askin'?" asks Lucas.

"She was a nutty lady on the hayride last night wearing all that ridiculous polka-dot clothing. Remember?" Tara lowers her voice immediately and looks to the ceiling, realizing her comments just might have been loud enough to carry upstairs to Carrie's room.

"I'm not sure. There wuz a lot of folks on the wagon last night."

"You cut off her head with a chainsaw." Tara is starting to flirt a bit. "Does that jog your memory a little? Ha-ha."

Lucas' face lights up. "Oh, yeah. *Her.*" He smiles and raises his hand high like he's holding her head by the hair again and shaking it in the air. Then he does a mock scary sound, "Ooh, arrgh."

They all have a good laugh at the parody, and when he raises his chipped coffee cup, he nods to each one like a hero accepting adulation from the masses. They all clink their cups and juice glasses together. *Bravo!* Tara waits until Lucas' eyes meet hers before she clinks with him.

"Well, so where is she? Wasn't she supposed to meet with us?"

"Wait! Dillon and I know. Remember I told you last night we took a selfie with her . . . well, with her dead body, anyway. Ha-ha. Here, let me show you. I charged my phone this morning."

Ma comes charging through the door again, and she bends down over his shoulder to look at the picture of Dillon and Josh in the maze at the operating table. She makes sure Lucas sees it too. "Look, Lucas, yer gittin' sloppy. They found where you do all yer killin'. Ha-ha. Look at her. I declare, I tol' y'all last night she looked a fright."

A sudden tinge of guilt comes over Dillon about the way they've been talking about Carrie. He'd been dismissive with Julia about her excessive worrying last night, but still, something is nagging at him. *Why isn't she here? Has something really happened to her? Not the head-chopping-off thing, of course, but something else? And here they were, making fun of her.*

"She *was* supposed to meet us this morning. Remember she had something *important* she had to tell us that just couldn't wait?" Tara uses air quotes with the word *important.*

Ma smiles a bit conspiratorially. "Oh, Missus Masterson? She had to go."

"All right, go Ma!" Tara raises her hand to give her a high-five, but Ma doesn't know what she's supposed to do, and they just fumble with their hands in the air. Her friends look away to keep from laughing.

Dillon is more interested in the facts. "She left? When? Last night?"

"Yeah, last night."

"I remember you said she looked terrible. Was that when she left?"

"Yeah, sometime around then," Ma says.

"Too bad. I wanted to see how the story was going to end," Dillon whines. There are giggles from all around, and then Ma goes back into the kitchen.

Josh turns to Lucas, "Hey, how did you do that head thing?"

"Jesus, Josh. Sometimes I wonder how you keep your job. Do we have to explain props to you?" Dillon feigns disgust but laughs.

"Well, you've done it a few times before anyway, right?"

"Oh yeah," boasts Lucas.

Everyone starts laughing again. Josh feels he's beginning to bond with Lucas a bit, and he secretly thinks it's pretty cool that he gets to play the villain on the hayride. "Hey, come over her, and I'll show you this game."

Tara changes the subject again and announces with a twinkle in her eye, "Okay, I want to pick some apples, *and* I want to see the corn maze––during the day. Then maybe it won't be so confusing when we go back again tonight."

"Lucas will be glad to show you around a bit this morning, won'tcha, Honeybee? The maze might have to wait till we close, though, but it'll be worth the wait, 'cuz he knows all the twists and turns. He made it, after all," Ma offers.

"Ma says Lucy 'n' me was born in a corn maze."

"So you are brother and sister of the corn, huh?" Dillon asks, assuming Lucas would get the reference. He was wrong.

"Ma says we might be twins!"

*Might be twins? How is it Ma doesn't know for sure?* Tara can't wait to tell her friends back home in her Ivory Tower about her adventure in a place where the people don't even know who their siblings are.

"It's gonna be a big day today fer us all," Ma interrupts. "Better git at it, Honeybee, we got a lot on our plates."

Great big Lucas reddens at being called Honeybee by Ma.

"Well, glad to meet you, Honeybee." Tara sticks out her hand to shake with Lucas. "The name's Tara, but you can call me Queen Bee." Ma's belly laugh is deep, and Lucas blushes again.

"Honeybee, why don't you go change an' put on yer nice shirt? We don't want the Queen Bee to think you's a hick now, do we?"

"Aw, Ma." When Lucas pushes back from the table and stands up, Josh takes a second to look him over. Lucas had been the hick bellboy, kind of a dumb guy who was unacquainted with Wi-Fi and didn't know the pleasures of video games. Now that his good friend Tara had chosen to include him in her day, in a sense she had brought him into their inner circle, and Josh is eager to find hidden assets to offset his obvious liabilities. Is his posture straighter than he remembers? He hadn't remembered those Hollywood cheekbones. *And his teeth . . . perfect and white!* Josh is nothing if not superficial.

"Give me five minutes an' I'll be ready, Tara."

"Wear that nice blue one we got the other day. Tag says Blueberry or something on it."

Nobody can see Tara crushing Josh's foot with her shoe. "I'll bet it says *Burberry*," Tara suggests.

"Um, huh? Okay." Lucas is already out of the dining room and headed down the back hall toward the private section of the house.

"Oh, never mind, I'll show you. I'm right behind ya, Honeybee." Ma dances out of the kitchen, so pleased at finally getting to play matchmaker for Lucas.

Josh starts to get up from the table. "I'll go with you guys too. Might as well get a tour of this . . ." but Dillon cuts him off.

"How about you and I stay here so that when your wife wakes up, she'll know that we all didn't just ditch her." Then he looks at Tara. "And why don't you two do what you want to do, and we'll meet up with you for lunch? What do you think—noon?"

Josh shuts up, realizing he's being stupid, and he sits back down. Tara gives him a coy little look and tries to buy a little more time. "Let's make that one o'clock."

"Screw that," Josh objects. "I'm not waiting around that long to eat lunch." This time it's Dillon who is kicking him under the table, and Josh winces. Now both feet hurt.

"Then don't eat with us, douchebag," Tara says, laughing at Josh as she leaves the room.

# 20

Tara and Lucas leaves the dining room to get dressed for their morning together; Lucas to put on something different, Tara to put on a little less. Ma's regular intrusions into each conversation and her hyperattentiveness to their every need require her to make constant entrances and exits through the kitchen's swinging door, and Dillon feels he's been a guest in a frantic episode of a television sitcom. Her departure from the scene has left a gaping hole in the room's ambience, and at the moment, both set and storyline have become unnervingly quiet.

The lazy tinkling sound Josh makes stirring his coffee with the tiny silver "I've been to South of the Border" teaspoon seems huge in this new silence. The two best friends have never needed to fill quiet spaces with a lot of conversation before to feel comfortable, but this time, Dillon wants to bring up the forbidden subject. Since Josh knows he does and doesn't want to go near it himself and since Dillon knows that Josh knows, they've both become a little jumpy, and sitting together in the quaint farmhouse dining room has become a little awkward.

Josh takes the first move to deflect what's coming. He bends down and peeks under the lacy white tablecloth, pretending to look for something. "Part of me still expects Polka Dots to show up, or maybe pop out from the shadows or crawl out from under the table."

"Ha-ha, very funny, Josh," humors Dillon. "But you can't get out of this. I want to know what the hell is going on between you and Julia. It seems to have gotten worse. Should I be worried?"

"I dunno, but can we talk about it somewhere else, maybe outside in a while? This house doesn't seem like a safe place to hold a private conversation."

"Sure, when?"

"I don't know. We can talk about it later. Right now I need to get some fresh air." Josh picks up his iPhone and heads out of the dining room.

# 21

It's sunny outside, and a lot warmer than Josh expected for late fall. By his own calculation, it must be at least the third Indian summer. Their late arrival yesterday limited what he could see of the farm to the black–and-white lens of the night, but this morning, like Dorothy waking up in Oz, everything outside is bursting in living color. Barns and outbuildings are festooned with rustic wreaths made out of vine, and Indian corn and bundles of giant cornstalks are lashed with huge colorful bows to the poles of massive tents. He notices some of the decorations appear a little worse for the wear, but didn't Ma say their pumpkin festival has been going on for five or six weeks?

Clearly this pumpkin thing is a big deal for the Winters. From the dozens of heavy picnic tables scattered around to the vast parking lot, everything looks designed to accommodate large crowds. Signage everywhere guides the masses: "Corn Maze this Way," "Pirate Ship that Way," "Port-a-Potties Over There," "Board Here for the Hayride."

They had considered spending that weekend at a number of other places, and until the standout entertainment last night, Josh had been skeptical about Winter's Farm and Orchard, even though Shelly had given it high marks. He is not above stereotyping, and the farm's location has made that easy. At home in the city, he and Julia wouldn't be caught dead in a restaurant that wasn't 'trending,' so the impressive infrastructure surrounding him is both gratifying and reaffirming. Their 'suite,' however, is appalling, and he is glad a room change is in the works before Julia starts in on him about it.

While the farm will not be open yet for a few more hours, the staff is already scurrying around. After a couple hundred people had rotated, tapped, and otherwise examined the pumpkins in front of the store the day before, today, younger kids are realigning the remaining ones into perfect rows and piles again. Others refill bins with little grotesque and ornamental squash. Teenagers are wiping off last night's rain from the displays that will hold the hundreds of bags of fresh apples customers wild buy today, and someone is already popping corn over near the store. It smells delicious. It is his last day to soak it all in, and Josh is psyched.

Just across the gravel driveway looms the famous apple orchard—at least that's what the sign says—"Farm and *Orchard*." But these apple trees didn't look like any apple trees he has ever seen before. These don't stand much taller than he does, and their branches stretch out flat against wires strung between posts in long rows. This orchard looks more like one of the many vineyards he and Julia had visited in Tuscany the year before. The misconception is not unique to him. During the tourist season, the Winters' nonstandard orchard requires daily explanations, and the level of detail they offer about the growing methods of the dwarf trees and the varieties of apples they grow, depends on how many times they've already had to say it before. It also depends upon their mood. Sometimes at the end of a day when visitors ask if that is their vineyard, they both find it easier just to say *yes*.

The apple trees aren't just in rows; they grow in rows and rows and rows in perfect alignment, with lush green grassy walkways between them. There is an almost architectural element to it. One or two rows are fascinating to see for the first time, but acres and acres of them are stunning. They fill his field of vision from left to right, and the left side stretches all the way to the front of the property.

About a vineyard they visited the year before in Tuscany, Josh had posted how he had felt they'd landed inside an oil painting by one of the great Italian masters. Now here they were again in a different but equally beautiful picture postcard setting. As he walks up to the trees for a closer examination and sees the branches are loaded with perfect apples, he thinks how fortunate he is to witness such beauty. He can't wait to share the orchard with Julia when she gets up. *Whenever that is going to be. She is always tired these days.*

Away from the orchard and in front of the store, Josh discovers a stage made out of an old hay wagon. According to the sign, a jug band will perform in a few hours, and he pictures happy families seated on the hay bales, applauding the fiddler or clapping for the banjo player as they wrap up their sets. Several little tents and booths where kids will sell concessions of one kind or another fill the space. On one of them, a red-and-green sign advertises "Fresh Apple Cider." After all he'd drunk the night before, he can't believe he's interested.

"Is this Ma's special cider?" he asks the gal setting up.

"Huh? What do you mean?

"You know, the hard stuff."

"Ah, we don't have nuthin' like that here. There's no drinking here at Winter's Farm and Orchard."

Josh pulls out a flask and gives the cider girl a wink before he takes a swig. "Really?"

"Sorry, sir. You'll have to put that away. Pa don't have no patience with alcohol."

"I can keep it a secret if you can."

# 22

Tara and Lucas stop at the Harvest Memories area of the farm. Grant Wood's *American Gothic* is by far the most popular, and they're just about to put their heads in the cutout when Josh shows up. "Come on, guys. Let me get a picture of you two. I might as well use my phone for something." They step behind the cutout and mimic the stern expressions of the famous couple in the real painting. Then Tara asks him to take another. This time she and Lucas switch positions, with Tara playing the part of the man and Lucas, the woman.

"I'll bet nobody's ever thought of doing that before," Josh teases. He takes a couple more shots, and when he's done, Tara makes Lucas come around to the front to preview the photos. They get a kick out of some, and of course they're horrified by others. "Delete that." "*Don't* delete that." "Look at *me*!" The only people not getting a kick out of their fun are the people patiently standing around waiting for them to get out of the way so they can have fun of their own.

Josh clears his throat behind a mischievous grin and speaks in a mock Appalachian accent, "Now ain't you two jest the spittin' image of a miserable married mister and missus?"

"Ma sez it ain't a husband and wife. S'pposed to be a farmer and his daughter."

"So? Out here, same difference, ha-ha. Right, Lucas?"

Lucas laughs along politely. "Um . . ."

"Good one, Josh. And I'll bet he's never heard that before either."

"Touché. Anyway, I'll send you both the pictures later. Well, at least I'll send them to you, Tara." Josh doesn't want to be a third wheel, and he makes his move to leave. "If I can ever get a signal, that is."

"*Touché?* Josh, who says that anymore? I swear . . ."

"You can come with us if you want," says Lucas.

"Hmm. Sounds like a plan. Maybe I . . ."

"Um. Lucas, weren't you going to show me that . . . thing?"

"Nah. Thanks." Josh figures it out. "You know what? I've got a thing I gotta see too."

A rustic handpainted sign points from the "Harvest Memory" area toward the Scary Giant Corn Maze. Tara reaches for Lucas's hand and whispers something to him. She gives her head a little tilt back to Josh and makes a girlish giggle as if to say, "See, Josh? So far, so good." He watches them long enough to see that Lucas does not seem that keen on reciprocating, but *oh well*, he'd called it. They're almost out of sight now, and Josh knows he's also out of her mind. He flashes them one final lonely smile they don't even see, and then he looks for a place to sit down alone.

# 23

"**S**eriously, a flask—already?" Josh can't tell if Dillon is being sarcastic or just plain judgmental. He's appeared out of nowhere and intruded upon his solitude, but he does not mind. Dillon had been his best friend for years.

"Don't start bitching at me." Josh shakes his head and pretends to get up and walk away.

"I was going to tell you I did speak with Jules last night, after everyone went to bed."

By now Josh expects to hear depressing news about his relationship with Julia. "So did she rake me over the coals?"

"We didn't talk at all about you, but I am, because your bickering is getting tiresome for the rest of us."

"Yeah, I know, and I'm sorry. It started with the kid thing, but it's escalated so even the most mundane issues erupt into nasty, snippy arguments. I had just gotten used to her serious mood swings, but now it seems she's always tired and sleeps a lot. I really don't know what to do."

"*The kid thing*—meaning you want to start having them now, and she's still not ready? I wonder why. Aside from being at each other's throats, I would think the timing couldn't be better for you two. You're almost a partner in the freaking firm now, for pete's sake. That's when hotshots like you are supposed to start families."

"I know, and she says she still does. I hope she means it. It's just that she's all over the place. One day she's thinking about getting back into fashion. Come on, fashion in DC? We already went down that route. Then she thinks she might try to put her expensive Georgetown English degree to use and write children's books. Children's books of all things! They both seem like pretty flimsy excuses to me, and I think there's something else going on she's not telling me. So what *did* you talk about then?"

"God, she was focused on that Carrie woman, and trying so hard to believe her story about sinister goings-on here at the farm."

"Oh, for Christ's sake! What's the matter with her?"

"So look, here's what she said, and Josh, she believes this. Okay, listen. So Shelly comes out here and runs into creepy Carrie and tries to get away from her as fast as she can. Then Ma, for some reason, has Shelly killed or something. Anyway, Shelly disappears, and Carrie finds out. Somehow Ma finds out that Carrie knows that she killed Shelly, so she arranges for Lucas to cut off Carrie's head with a chainsaw, basically in front of everyone. And before she gets murdered, Carrie yells out Shelly's name so Julia can put the pieces of this puzzle together."

"Maybe she should write murder mysteries."

"Ha-ha. She always did have a pretty active imagination."

"I just discovered she's taking sleeping pills. Found her bottle in the bathroom this morning. How come I didn't know this before?"

Dillon puts his hand on Josh's shoulder. "I want kids too. Did I ever tell you that?"

"No."

"Course it's going to be a little trickier for me, you know, the woman part. Maybe next year."

"What do you mean? You finally met someone up to your standards?"

"No. But thanks for reminding me I'm a loser. Now give me your damn flask."

As he turns to hand Dillon his flask, Josh catches sight of Lucy crouching behind a tree, trying to hide. He shakes his head. "What's with that goofy chick, anyway?" He turns to her. "Hey, Lucy, are you stalking me or something? See, I told you we were going to have trouble finding a place to talk privately."

Lucy's cover is blown. She immediately stands up straight and pretends to be doing something important to the tree she'd used to hide behind, but all she can think to do is to kind of wipe the trunk with one of her hands. When she realizes how unconvincing that is, she toddles off toward the house. Josh takes another swig from his flask and calls after her. "And find me some Internet, okay?" He looks for a hay bale and sits down.

"How did you decide it wasn't working with Rick?"

"Josh, my situation with Rick was totally different."

"How so?"

Dillon hesitates, "There wasn't much to it. We had different ideas about how committed we wanted to be to each other, so I dumped him."

"It was that easy?"

"Of course not, but commitment's something you want to agree on." Dillon leans closer to him. "You have something completely different with Jules."

"Do I? Seems to me we have the same problem."

"You have to put yourself in your partner's place before you decide anything life-altering."

"Did you do that with him?" Josh questions.

"I tried."

"What did you see when you did?" Josh says, looking up at a small black bird flying over the farm.

"It doesn't matter what I saw with Rick. It only matters what you see with Jules. Come on, buddy. Let's walk around and have some fun."

# 24

It's just after eleven o'clock, and the parking lot is already filling up. One of the little kids with the burlap heads is directing the traffic, and Josh and Dillon are impressed. When one long row gets filled, the kid runs back to the beginning of the row and waves the next cars to line up in a second row in perfect alignment behind the first. They're also impressed how he stands up to some of the big guys in big trucks who don't want to follow his orders and try to park any way they want.

*Vroom vroom.* Their fascination in the parking lot system is interrupted by the sound of a powerful engine revving up, and it appears to be coming from a tall windmill-like contraption at the edge of the orchard. The blades sit atop an impressive tower that at one time must have been painted a sort of industrial-silver color, perhaps for the benefit of low-flying aircraft at night. Today, though, its original coat is chipped, faded, and a little blotchy, and the blades that are rotating in slow motion at the top don't look like those of a traditional windmill. They look more like propellers of an airplane.

A shiny new object commands their attention, and they're on their feet in seconds to check it out. As they near the windmill, they can tell the action is happening inside a rickety wooden wall that surrounds the tower's base. Josh is reaching for the handle to open the gate, when the gate swings open instead and knocks into him.

Pa steps out, tool belt jingle-jangling. "Sorry about that, son. Sumthin' you want?"

"We heard the noise and thought we'd see what's going on," Dillon explains. "I love engines."

"That's quite a windmill you got," Josh adds.

"This ain't no windmill, boy. It's a wind *machine.*"

"A wind machine? What's it fer . . . for?"

"It's like one of them fans that rotates all the way in a circle, ya see, blowin' air 'round a room, 'cept this big ol' thing blows air over all them apple trees. We crank her up when we think there's gonna be a frost. She's cantankerous, so while the weather's nice, I'm gittin' 'er ready fer when we need 'er come spring." When he leans in close to Josh, Pa's boozy blast of moonshine almost knocks him over. "You oughta see them blades spin when she's hummin', boy. I reckon they'd slice through a man's bones like a knife through butter. But up there's the best view of the farm and the ridge, an' you kin see everything. Lemme know if you want to climb up sometime, sometime when it's not running, that is. He-he."

"Well, I sure would like to!" Dillon shouts over the engine noise. "I'm kind of a daredevil, so . . ."

Pa looks Dillon up and down and snickers a little. "Hmm. You, a daredevil? Now ain't that sumthin'. Well, anyhow, it's an easy climb up that ladder. You put on one of these here belts. They got a strap, see? An' a hook you clip on the rungs of the ladder as you go up, safe as can be. See? I got one on now."

"Okay, yeah. Great. How about later?" Josh asks.

"Yeah, later." Pa spits off to his side and goes back to rev up the engine again. Dillon and Josh are captivated by this fascinating contraption Pa calls a wind machine. It's a little sci-fi and oddly low-tech, and they can't wait to post their pictures posing with their new find.

"I think I need more coffee," Dillon announces, as he closes the gate behind them on the way out.

"Check on Julia, will you? I'm going to walk around some more."

"Sure."

# 25

**D**illon is back in the dining room reading the paper when Ma enters. "No plans for the day, dear?" she asks Dillon.

"Oh, I've already been out this morning. Right now I'm just waiting on my friend to wake up."

"Mrs. Peale? Well, you're quite the gentleman, ain't you? You'll make some lady a fine husband one day."

Dillon sighs and returns a smile before continuing to read the column in this poor excuse for a newspaper, where people apparently are encouraged to write in to complain about everything. "Oh, yes, ma'am. I just haven't found the right girl yet."

She is trying to determine if Dillon is being snarky with her, when they both snap their heads up to the ceiling. Someone upstairs is screaming her head off.

"*Julia!*"

\* \* \*

"Jules, what's wrong? What happened?" Dillon asks breathlessly from the hallway. He's turning the doorknob back and forth, thinking if he does it enough times it will open. He looks back at Ma. "Can't you get in? Don't you have a key or something?"

Ma fumbles with her ring of keys, and this time it seems to take forever to find the right one. Just as she's about to turn the giant key, Julia unlocks the door and opens it from the inside. She's wearing a bathrobe. She's been crying and looks terrible.

"Everything all right, dearie? My heart jumped plumb out of my chest and into the kitchen when I heard you holler."

"No. No, everything's not all right." Julia is frantic. "I've been raped!"

# 26

The farm is packed, and Josh finds a spot in the orchard where he can be away from people yet still see what's going on. He takes another swig. To the left, he watches the rows stretch all the way to the horizon, and when he brings his gaze back all the way to the right, he's face-to-face with one of the burlap boys.

"Pretty spooky mask you guys wear," he says at the kid. "Hey, are you the one I saw last night playing out in the road? I can't tell, you guys all look alike, ha-ha." The kid remains mute, but Josh can see his eyes staring out at him from behind the slits in his mask. It's a little unnerving, because the kid doesn't move either. "So how old are you?" Nothing. A strong hand clamps down on Josh's shoulder. He jumps and whips around. Pa! How did he not hear that jingle-jangling tool belt?

"A mite early to be imbibing, ain't it, son?"

Josh looks down at his sterling silver flask, a gift from Julia. "Um. You mean this . . ."

"There ain't no alcohol allowed here at the festival."

"What? How can you have a festival without alcohol?" Josh protests.

"Sorry, but them's the rules." Pa is in the process of rolling another cigarette, which he will place in the exact same spot on his dried-up old lips, where there is always one dangling. "We run a nice, clean God-fearing family operation here, son, an' we don't want no bad influences on the kids."

"Oh." Josh holds up the flask. "Good to know, but this is water."

"I ain't no fool, young man. You kin smell the liquor on ya two farms over." Pa looks mean and crude and a little frightening.

*Look who's talking!* Josh wonders why Pa's cigarettes don't spontaneously combust. "Come on, man. I'm not bothering anyone. And what about last night? Your cider is hardly nonalcoholic."

"Night's night, and day's day, an' yer smart enuf to know the difference. There's children here. Impressionable children." He takes a long drag on his cigarette.

"Okay, fine. Your farm, your rules. I get it." Josh backs down. He screws the cap back onto the flask and puts it away. "Happy now?"

"We've got our eyes on you, young man."

Josh bristles, and he's just about to say something stupid when Pa starts to chuckle and pokes him in the ribs. "Oh, I'm just foolin' with you, boy. He-he. But ya better sober up if you and yer friend are wantin' to climb up my wind machine later. It kin be dangerous."

"You got it, Pa." He's relieved.

The tool belt seems to be jingling louder than ever, and it occurs to him that maybe sneaking up on him was part of the joke. As soon as Pa turns down one of the cross paths and is out of sight, Josh turns and sticks his tongue out at the kid. No reaction.

# 27

Julia stammers through uncontrollable tears. "Someone came in my room last night. They took off my clothes and raped me. My clothes aren't here, so they must have taken them. I have to tell Josh, and we need to get the hell out of here right away."

"Raped? Oh my god! Who did it?"

"That's the trouble. I don't know who did it."

"Now how could that be, child? Why you wuz locked up tight in here. Lemme take a look around fer yer clothes."

Julia is panicky, and Dillon tries to get her to sit down. "So when did it happen? Start from the beginning."

Looking at Dillon, she stammers, "I'm not sure exactly. Last night, when Ma left me in here, I locked the door and fell into bed with my clothes on. I know I did. When I woke up this morning, I was naked."

"Okay, but when did the rape happen?"

While Julia started to recount the nightmare of her night, Ma was rummaging around in Julia's dresser, and she interrupts to redirect the conversation. "Say, aren't these what you wuz wearin last night? I think so, see? Here's that pretty blue top you had on. And those nice blue jeans and these whatchamacallits. You folded 'em all nice and put 'em away proper after all," Ma says brightly.

"Huh? I did? Yes, of course they're mine."

Dillon looks over at Ma, and they share troubled frowns.

"Now I don't want to say none of this happened, but sometimes that cider of ours can make for some wild dreams. You wuz startin' to imagine things before you went to sleep. And with the storm and all . . ."

Julia shakes her head and looks up at Dillon for support. "Look, I don't know about the clothes, but a woman can tell when she's had sex, you know, and I know I was raped. Somebody else was in my bed. Look there's dirt on the sheets." The situation is clearly awkward for both of them.

"You know last night you wuz on the hay wagon, and from what I heard, there wuz hay flying every which way. In the corn maze too. Probably got some dirt on ya."

"And I smell like gasoline. Here, smell! There wasn't any gasoline on the hayride." Julia can't look at herself.

"No, Julia, you smell just fine. And believe me, I know the smell of gasoline. You said you locked yer door, so how do you s'ppose sumbody got in here, now?" Ma is speaking very compassionately, but the expression she conveys to Dillon says *We both know that would have been impossible.*

"I did lock the door. I got up to lock it. Maybe I'm confused a little, but I know I was raped. Anyway, we're getting out of here. Ma, please call the police." Julia is becoming a little threatening. "And get me a doctor too!"

"Yes, of course. I'm so sorry 'bout all this. Let me bring you up some breakfast, and while yer eatin', I'll call for the sheriff to come out with ol' Doc Starnes. You can explain everything to them."

"Thank you."

"But just so you know—and I guess you didn't—well, um, I guess ol' Ma is gonna have to tell you in front of yer friend here. Yer husband was up walkin' around in the middle of the night. Kept us all up with all the bed squeakin' an' commotion an' all coming from your room, if ya know what I mean."

"Josh?"

"Yes, indeed. Quite a man he is too, from the sounds of it. Jest thought you should know before you start accusing people to the good sheriff and wasting Doc Starnes's time an' all."

# 28

On the way to the Scary Giant Corn Maze, Tara and Lucas pass a spacious playground that takes up about a quarter acre of woods and lawn. There is a wooden train with a locomotive, a coal car, a couple of freight cars, and a club car, all big enough for little kids to play in and around and on, but the biggest attraction by far is the pirate ship.

"A pirate ship in the middle of a farm! Who would have guessed?" In Tara's quest to seduce Lucas, she marvels at everything he shows her.

"We used to play on this when we wuz young'uns."

The hulk of the huge wooden ship with three decks, a formal boarding ladder, and a curvy slide looks like it has been stranded in a permanent low tide in the play area on the farm. Even though now it is surrounded by a thick layer of mulch instead of raging seas, the Winter's Farm pirate ship proudly flies the skull and crossbones above her wheelhouse. Pumpkin pirates manned the decks, and there was a foreboding pumpkin pirate captain at the helm. There were even smaller pumpkin pirate kids sitting and hanging on branches of the trees surrounding the ship. In just two days, it will temporarily lose its commission again and assume the status of "ghost ship," but today hundreds of kids will board, pilot, push, shove, slide down its pole, and walk its plank.

"Do you really make all these pumpkin people all yourself, Lucas?"

"Yeah. Well, this ship has always been one of my favorite places in the farm, and I'm certain it's why I have a passion for everything pirate-related. It makes me feel good to see all the little kids enjoying it too. I'm thinking of building another ship to put over there, but that will mean I'll have to install cannons on this one, though, to protect it from the new invader."

Tara looked stunned. Thirty seconds ago, she had been doing her best to play the coquette, but now her face reflected the seriousness of an academic. She looked him directly in his face. "Lucas, what happened to your accent?"

"Accent? *Uh-oh.* Did I do it again? I didn't even notice I had switched."

"What do you mean, 'do it again'? Is this your normal voice?"

"I don't know. Sometimes it just comes out, although I'm not sure why. Please don't tell Ma. She doesn't want me to speak like this in front of the guests."

"This is so fascinating, Lucas. Listen, I've got a colleague, a linguist at MIT, where I teach. I know he'd want to interview you for a paper he's working on about code switching or something. Would you mind if I gave him your name?"

"I don't know, Tara. I don't mind helping you, but I don't know how we could do it without Ma finding out."

"Let's see if we can't figure out a way. How about that?" Tara is now more intrigued than ever with her new young friend, and she's starting to believe he may be more diamond than rough after all. She puts her arm around his waist, and when he doesn't respond, she takes his arm and places it around her waist. After humoring her for a few seconds, he pulls it back and checks the time. He's wearing a Rolex, and Tara can tell that it's real. Batting her eyes, she tilts her head back a bit in her most coquettish attempt yet. "You are so full of surprises, Lucas Winter."

"He-he." He pauses. "What do you mean?"

"The Rolex."

"The what?" Lucas looks all around him.

"On your wrist, the Rolex. It's a little unexpected, that's all."

"Oh, the watch. Is that how you pronounce it? Rolex? I think I've been saying it wrong for a whole year." He turns to lead her away from the ship.

"Aren't we going to see the ship?"

"You can come back to it later, but if we're going to see some of the corn maze, we'll have to head over there now, because I have a lot to do later today."

"Well, dern it then. We best git to the maze," Tara teases.

Lucas leads her across a broad lawn and follows the little signs to the Scary Giant Corn Maze. To avoid waiting in the long line at the entrance, Lucas leads her in a secret way.

# 29

Josh has left Pa's noisy and cantankerous wind machine far behind him in exchange for something completely different. He isn't ready to return to the house and decides to explore the tall woods he saw on the other side of the farm for a while instead. *Now these are real trees.* An inviting old oak catches his eye, and fashioning a pile of pine needles and dry leaves into a nice fat cushion beneath it, he leans back in great luxury, with only a slight breeze and the occasional plop of another acorn falling to the ground to keep him company. *Perfect. Well, almost.* He pulls out his iPhone and swipes to his newest obsession. Of all the games he's been addicted to, Pumpkin Menace is his favorite. Now that he is a busy Washington, DC, attorney, he doesn't have a lot of free time. He really isn't much of a gamer anymore, but this game is fun and requires focus, and it is perfect right now to take his mind off his difficult marriage.

He's been playing for about thirty minutes when he hears a couple of twigs snap behind him. He is up to ninety-eight pumpkins, so there is a lot at stake, and he doesn't look up from his phone. But he feels he can at least speak. "Hello? Anybody there?" Silence. A few minutes later, more twigs snap, and now something is making a lot of noise in the dry leaves. A couple of birds he wouldn't have been able to identify call out a warning.

"Is that you, Polka Dots? I keep thinking you're going to show up. Ha-ha. Damn! Look what you made me do!"

Deciding he probably needs to take a break anyway, he stands up to see what is making the noise, and since there doesn't appear to be any other humans in his neck of the woods, he concludes that a small animal must have been the culprit that disturbed his peace and broke his running streak. There is no breeze anymore, and everything has become eerily quiet. He gets quiet too and decides to figure out the source of the noise by focusing his vision on small sections of the woods. It's so quiet; he's becoming a little panicky because now he's worried it might not be a small animal after all, and he can feel his heart slamming against his chest. When the squirrel bounds out noisily from behind him and scampers up a tree, he jumps.

*Whew! Jesus Christ, Josh. You need to relax.*

As Josh turns around to resume his spot at the base of the oak tree, Leatherface is staring him in the face. "Holy shit! How did you get here?" He stumbles back, trips on a rock, and catches himself before nearly falling to the ground. He must look like an idiot, and Leatherface agrees, because he makes Josh his creepy cackling laugh before lumbering away.

"Hey! Fuck you for scaring me, asshole!"

Leatherface whips back around. *Whap!* He nails Josh in the chest with a cow pie.

"The fuck?"

It only takes a second to figure out what hit him. "You son of a bitch! What the hell was that for?" He takes off after Leatherface without considering what he's going to do when he catches him, but it's moot when he trips on a tree root and falls spread-eagle on the ground.

# 30

**M**a has left to make some breakfast for Julia, while Dillon is sitting with her at a small round table in front of the window of her very large bedroom. Despite the seriousness of the situation, Dillon can't help making comparisons between their rooms. The furnishings in his room are perfectly fine—they're plain, yet every detail in this room is lovely, down to the pretty antique jacquard tablecloth in front of him. Julia said it had been reserved for Shelly, and he wonders how she had rated this great room. Furthermore, since she didn't even show up, why didn't Ma offer it to one of them? He stops being envious for a moment. "Do you remember anything else about last night?"

Julia had been animated and emotional when they first got to her room, but now with Dillon there for support, she has become less frantic. "You didn't see the tiny bed we have in our room. It's unbelievable. I was so exhausted, but I just couldn't get comfortable, so I got up and was going to crash on the sofa in that little room off the front hall." She gestures to the room downstairs. "But Ma found me."

On cue again, Ma enters the room, carrying a tray with two mugs. She brings the hot chocolate in an old aluminum thermos with a red rubber stopper. Under the circumstances, Dillon has been taking the situation seriously and has dropped his comic persona, so rather than make a funny comment to Ma, he simply nods to acknowledge the tray. He has to struggle a little with the stopper, though, and it is difficult to resist trying his teeth. He pours a mug of cocoa for each of them, and Julia downs hers as soon as it is cool enough to swallow.

"When Ma found me downstairs, she offered me hot cocoa."

Dillon watches the steam rise from his mug.

"She told me it was some kind of special cocoa that would help me sleep." She takes another long drink from her cup. "But I remember it was delicious. Like this."

He stops staring at his mug and pushes it off to the side without ever tasting it. "What happened then?"

Julia is staring out the window. "I don't know. That's when it gets a little hazy. She brought me up here, and then it all kind of went blank."

Dillon shoots a look across the room to where Ma is pacing and then back at Julia. He grabs the mug out of Julia's hand before she can drink any more of it.

"Dillon! What are you doing?"

He leans across the table and starts to whisper a mile a minute. "Okay, so you were fine. Then you drank some *special hot cocoa*, and then you blacked out. Jesus, do you think Ma was trying to poison you?"

"It wasn't Ma and the cocoa, Dillon," she responds, not whispering. From across the room, Ma pretends to be occupied.

"How do you know?"

He waits for a response. None comes.

"You said it all happened after you had the cocoa, right?"

"Right."

"Could someone else have put anything in your drink? Think!"

"Now, young man, I see where this is going." Ma charges over to the table to defend herself. "There weren't nobody but the young lady and me alone in the kitchen last night. And don't you fret none, there ain't nothing wrong with the cocoa I just brought you. I seen you ain't touched yers."

"No, Dillon. Ma is right. The cocoa wasn't the problem. I was just exhausted, and . . ."

Dillon interrupts her. "Wait a minute. I don't care how tired you were. People just don't pass out on their own, and if the hot chocolate—"

"Ahem," Ma interrupts. "Well, young lady, are you going to tell him, or should I?" Ma knows she's not going to be implicated in all this, but she wants to be sure Dillon knows where the real blame lies.

"It wasn't the hot chocolate, Dillon," she insists.

"That's what you keep saying. Then what was it?" he asks again. Silence. He looks over at Ma. "How come Ma knows something I don't know?"

"All right, I'll tell you."

Ma turns now to leave, and on her way out, she mutters, "I think my work here is done."

"I've been having problems sleeping, okay? I've been taking some pills for it, and last night, I might've taken more than I was supposed to." She's still staring out the window. "And I might be on some other medications too. Please don't tell Josh."

"Other medications, Jules? I won't, but why won't you?" Dillon seems concerned.

Julia rolls her eyes. "Because it's not a big deal, but he'll turn it into one."

"Yeah, you're probably right, but are you supposed to be drinking booze with these other so-called medications?"

Julia is quiet but then speaks. "No, of course not. And they're antidepressants. There! That's why I wasn't drinking the cider at first last night. You all made such a big deal about it, I finally gave in."

Dillon sighs a little. "I'm sorry, Jules. You know I would have supported you if I'd known. I'm just glad the Winters aren't psychos after all." He pauses. "And now that we've established you weren't raped, do you think the rest of what happened might just have been the pills and booze talking? And the cocoa?"

Julia deliberately ignores his question. "Look at that scarecrow over there."

Dillon follows her gaze. "Jules, are you listening to me?"

"Yes, maybe."

"Yes—maybe you're listening, or yes—maybe you imagined it?"

"Yes, both, maybe, but I still want to get out of here." She stops talking and just stares. "It looks like that scarecrow is wearing Carrie's hat. What do you think?" She stands up halfway to get a better look. "Could that be Carrie's polka-dot beret?"

He stands a little to get a better look, and he has to squint too. "I don't know, it's hard to tell from here."

"Oh come on, Dillon. Of course it's hers. How many polka-dot berets have you seen in your life? And how did hers get on that scarecrow over there?"

"I don't know. Maybe she put it there herself. Look, we've got enough going on right now without rehashing her story again."

Julia glances to the clock on the fireplace mantle. It's eleven thirty. "She told me to meet her at ten."

"Well, that can hardly be her fault. You slept till after eleven."

"But did anybody see her at breakfast?"

"Not that I know of."

"I never got to her last night. She tried to warn me, and I never followed up. Can you try to find her and see if she's OK? I'd feel terrible if anything happened to her."

"I'd like to help you, but she's not here. Ma said she had to go, so I don't think we're likely to run across her now."

"All right then, see if you can get her phone number from Ma. She must have it, and she likes you. Will you promise me, Dillon?"

"Yes, of course. Now do you still want me to go get Josh? It's going to take me a while to find him."

"Yes, please. And find Tara too, OK?"

Julia interrupts his departure by motioning him to come back over to her.

"What is it? I've got to get going."

"Shh." She motions for him to come even closer. "And last night, something weird was going on down in the basement. I'd like you to check on it too."

*Here we go again.*

Julia tells Dillon about the basement door and the room full of dolls, and while he is fascinated, he's not swallowing the whole story. "So I'm not saying there wasn't a woman in the basement crying for help, but given what we know what happened, isn't it possible something else down there might have been making noises that you thought sounded like a voice?" Dillon is trying very hard to be gentle with his friend.

"I suppose, but then there was this loud clanking that must have come from the furnace coming on, and I got scared and had to leave before I could find out anything for sure."

When Ma enters the room again, she is prepared to take charge of both Julia and the situation. "All right, sweet precious thing, I called the sheriff and Doc Starnes, and they'll both be out soon. Dillon here is finally going to go out to find your adorable husband, aren't you? An' while we're waiting, maybe you'd like to lie down again."

"No, what I'm going to do right now is take a nice long hot shower in my private bathroom and wash off everything to do with this horrible place."

"Oh, dearie. I'm so sorry it had to end this way. Why don't I draw you a nice bath instead?"

# 31

Josh is wandering the woods trying to figure out why Leatherface was being so hostile, when he hears more rustling sounds. *Not again.* He turns around. "Hey, fuck you, you punk. You want to throw shit at me again? Try it!" Josh looks around in every direction, but there's no one in sight, until he spins back around and sees the burlap boy standing about ten feet away. "Jesus, kid. You again? You've got to stop scaring me, okay?" *These people come from out of nowhere!*

As usual, the child doesn't speak. "Hey, sorry about my language by the way. You should get back to the festival. There's a real sicko out here."

No reaction. "Come on. We'll go back together." Josh steps toward the kid and offers him a hand, when the boy suddenly takes off into the woods.

# 32

Dillon leaves Julia's room and is not quite sure what to do. Tara is out with Lucas and isn't due back for a couple hours, and who knows where Josh is by now? Ma and Dillon agree Julia needed a nice long rest, but he decides to start looking for Josh anyway.

At the bottom of the stairs, he remembers his promise to Julia and turns back down the hall to check out the basement door. He jiggles the doorknob, but it doesn't open. It's not locked, just bolted at the top. She said she heard noises down there coming from machinery of some kind, a pump or something. *So what? A basement in a house like this is probably full of noisy old contraptions.* He runs his fingers lightly over the door as he replays her adventure from the night before. Then he remembers the part where she fell back onto the wall and knocked down a picture. Looking at the wall behind him, though, there's no empty nail or missing picture. Either they've already replaced the one she broke, or it never happened. Both possibilities make perfect sense to him.

Standing there in the quiet hallway, Dillon wondered what he should fear most—what might be going on in the basement, or what might be going on with Julia. He gets an idea and drops to his hands and knees. If her story *is* right, there might still be some broken glass on the floor. Seems like there's always one more little piece of glass you can't sweep up the first time. He's brushing his hands flat along the floor, when *bam!* Another door somewhere down the hall slams shut again. It startles him, and when he jerks his hand away, he gets a splinter in his index finger. "Crap!" *What's with all the doors slamming in this house?* His mood grows dark when the splinter appears to be a piece of glass. Instinctively he puts his finger in his mouth.

The door slam announces the arrival of Lucy, looking ridiculous in an old-fashioned maid's uniform. She's toting a mop, a broom, a bucket, and an ancient upright vacuum cleaner. It's a tight squeeze to get around Dillon in the narrow hallway, and the broom handle knocks into him and clatters to the floor. When she stoops to pick up the broom, she manages to lose her mop, and they both have to do a bit of a two-step to make enough room for her to collect all her gear and pass by each other.

As he heads back to the front hall foyer, he runs into Ma. "Whatcha doing back here? Is there sumthin' I can get you? I thought you wuz goin' to go look fer Julia's husband. An' what happened to yer finger?"

"Oh nothing, just a splinter. I was going to see if Julia had a set of tweezers I could borrow before I went looking for Josh."

"Nuthin doin'. You come right in and sit back down, and I'll take care of it. You don't know how many of those things I've pulled out of folks on this here farm. Just so happens, I've got a needle and tweezers right here." Ma pulls him into the room with the dolls and opens a drawer in a chest. After a few moments of digging around, she extracts a pincushion and a set of glasses. "This used to be a sewing room before it became the *nursery*."

"Ah, so this is the room Julia was talking about." *Well, she was right about the room. It's pretty weird, and she calls this her nursery.*

In seconds, Ma is sitting on an old platform rocking chair, and with one swift motion, she pins his outstretched arm on her lap, locking his hand in a death grip he never saw coming. Under the light of a gooseneck floor lamp, she examines Dillon's index finger. How the stiff bulge of Scotch tape kept the two halves of her magnifying glasses together he'll never know, but Ma is clearly ready to operate.

"I can't look!" He strains to look away from the surgery and the surgeon. "Ouch!"

"Got it!" she announces with a flourish. She releases him and stands up and rushes across the hall to a small powder room. You can hear the water rushing in the sink. "Should a been a nurse," she mumbles.

"Was it a big piece of glass?"

"Glass? Now glory, why would ya think it wuz glass? Just a nice shiny white splinter. Matched the white from our baseboard." Ma is shouting from inside the bathroom over the noise of the water splashing. "You wuzn't down on our floor now, wuz you? Ha-ha."

"Can I see it?"

"What, the splinter? Too late, it went down the drain. Now shouldn't you be out lookin' fer yer friend? You made me call for the sheriff, remember? He should be here before long."

\* \* \*

In spite of the multiple traumas to her body, mind and spirit, Julia enjoyed soaking in the luxurious tub in the private bath off her room. The deep tub, the bath salts, and the Jacuzzi jets were just what she needed, and she started to realize there was really no reason to rush things either. After all, the sheriff would take care of everything. She sank back down and closed her eyes. *Maybe I'll rest for just a minute.*

# 33

I t is a big farm, and there are crowds of people and long lines everywhere, and Dillon knows it is not going to be as easy as he thought to find Josh. He decides to approach his search systematically, one area at a time, and he'd start looking with the Pumpkin Patch. But first he makes a slight detour to check out the scarecrow they saw from Julia's window, the one wearing the beret. He sees that it is set back from the edge of the corn and a little taller than most of the other Pumpkin People, but he thinks he can still get close enough to remove it. He reaches with his arm and needs to jump up high a couple of times before he can even touch it. The hat appears only to be sitting on the pumpkin head and not attached to it, so he thinks he can probably snatch it if he can just get a little more height. He backs away and takes a running start, as though he is making a layup. *Wfft! Success!* Now he wonders what it is going to tell him exactly.

*Blood.* The whole headband of the beret is caked with blood, and there's more spattered on the top. Blood dots on top of polka dots. "Shit!" Dillon drops it like it is on fire, and he kneels down to wipe his hand over and over in the thick grass. *The sheriff is definitely going to want to see this!* But he needs something to pick it up with. He's definitely not going to touch it again. *A napkin!* He races toward main area in front of the store and barrels through the crowds to the front of the line at the Whoopi Pie booth. He's about to ask for a couple, when some of the folks at the back of the line take exception to his cutting in front of them. "Hey, boy, out here we all wait our turns."

"Yes, of course, I'm sorry, but it's an emergency. There's something I can't touch with my hands, and I need—"

"Hey, the end of the line is back here, city boy!" shouts someone else, a little less politely.

Dillon reluctantly goes to the end of the line to wait his turn, and while he is standing there, he scans the area for a stand with a shorter line. Nobody seems to want veggie burgers, and he dashes over there, grabs a bunch of napkins and a paper plate for good measure, and heads back toward the scarecrow. By now, several groups and families are using the walkway along the same outside edge of the maze, and they obscure the scarecrow, which makes it difficult for him to find his reference point.

When the first of the large families finally passes, there is enough of a gap before the next group for him to spot the hat where he left it on the ground. *There it is!* He takes off after it, but he's too slow. A little girl sees the beret first and picks it up. "Look what I found!" she says, as she models it on her head, oblivious to the blood. She's showing it off to her friends, when her vigilant mother notices and whips it right off her head. "Heather, you don't know where that hat's been!" With one dismissive swing, she flings the beret like a Frisbee up into the air, and Dillon is disheartened to watch it sail over the tips of the corn and land somewhere deep in the thick cornfield.

"Waa!" the little girl cries.

"Stop your crying now or I'm going to call your father over."

*Crap! Now it's going to take forever to find it again.* As Dillon heads toward the general area where he thought it landed, he is overcome by a horrible revelation. That simple exchange between mother and daughter has helped connect some dots. *Call your father over.* He wondered how Ma could have called the sheriff if the phone line was *fried*, as he remembers her describing it? *Uh-oh.* Dillon decides finding the beret can wait. First, he has to find Josh and Tara, and then he has to go back to warn Julia. The girl's mother has no idea why the nice young man racing past her yells "Thank you!" to her, and because she doesn't know who he is, she scowls back at him.

# 34

"**G**osh, all this hiking is making me hot. You look a little hot too. Are you?" No response. "Are you, Lucas, just a little?" she asks again.

Lucas is staring at his watch.

They've been walking around for a long time—in circles, for all she knows—and nothing Tara tried has succeeded in getting Lucas even a little bit romantic. She's been vacillating between thinking it probably isn't worth all the effort she is putting forth and making it her personal challenge. Besides, the articulate side of Lucas still intrigues her. But she has only one trick left in her book. She pulls off her cashmere sweater and hangs it temporarily on a nearby scarecrow. *What the hell. Desperate times, desperate measures. If he doesn't like me in this cute T-shirt, I give up!* She is about to walk back over to pick up her sweater in defeat, when she notices the Pi Phi hoodies she and Julia saw the night before. "Lucas, look at this. It's a hoodie from my sorority. Julia and I saw it in here last night. Do you know how it got here? I can't imagine a sister would have left it on purpose."

Tara fingers the inside collar of the jersey and finds a tag. "Oh my god! Look at this! I'd recognize it anywhere. *Shelly Roberts!* We all made the same tags for our clothes that year. Do you know who I'm talking about? She was the friend who was supposed to be here yesterday! What the hell is going on?"

"A very nice lady was wearing it a few days ago. Ma told us the woman had to go, and I guess she must not have come back for it. I remember Lucy wanted it, but I told her my pumpkin people always came first."

"But Ma told us Shelly never showed up here. Why would she say that? Something's not right. Sorry, but I've got to get back and see what the others think. Can I take this?"

"Certainly." A little vibrating sound catches her attention, and she is surprised when she sees the small PDA he has unclipped from his belt.

"What's that, a pager?"

"Yes, Ma likes gadgets, and this way she can keep in touch with us at all times."

"That definitely qualifies as a gadget. I didn't know you could still get them," she says, shaking her head in disbelief.

*Beep.* "Um, Ma needs me right away. I have to help get someone out of the maze. I'm sorry, but I really have to go. Remember, please don't tell her."

"What about helping *me* get out of the maze? I'll go with you."

"Sure, OK, but I've gotta go fast. It's some kinda emergency. Follow me, and keep up if you can."

He sets an ambitious pace, and Tara is able to keep up, but for being in such a big hurry, she thinks he's taking a pretty circuitous route. *He must know what he's doing. He said he could get out from anywhere in three and a half minutes.* The sun has dried the ground of the wider main paths they've been on so far, but the paths he is picking for their quick way out are narrower and narrower. In no time, they are not on a real path at all. She slept through most of last night's storm, but now she is beginning to appreciate how much rain had fallen. The ground is soaked and muddy, and it is getting worse. It reminds her of an uncomfortable trek she'd made through the Amazon jungle with a guy. It hadn't worked out with him either.

The mud slows her pace to a crawl, and after five minutes or so of slipping and sliding, one of her feet sinks into some deep muck and won't come out. She holds on to a brittle cornstalk for support, and as she strains to pull her foot out, it makes an ugly sucking sound. *Where the hell is Lucas?* Ultimately, the recalcitrant mud isn't willing to release the shoe, only her foot. *Shit! They were expensive!* Now it is even more of a struggle to yank the shoe out, because she is standing on one leg with one bare foot in the air. The vacuum created by the mud is stronger than she thought, but the corn stalk isn't, and when it breaks, she collapses into the brittle corn. Her expensive jeans are covered with sloppy muck, but she manages to retrieve her shoe. Now they match. "Lucas! Slow down. Hey, this isn't funny." *He is going to owe me big-time tonight.* From far away in the corn, Tara hears his apology. "Sorry, catch you later."

*Okay. He had to go, I get it. My fault. Dumb shoes to wear out here. What was I thinking?* With her guide out of sight, she begins to panic but not about where she is. She knows exactly where she is. She is all alone in the mud in the middle of a stupid cornfield, and it is going to take her a long time to find her way out.

# 35

J osh sprints through the woods in hot pursuit of the boy. "Damn it, kid! I'm trying to help you!" But it's a waste of breath, and the kid keeps running. Josh weaves around trees and hurdles fallen branches and is just within arm's reach, when he's jerked backward and slams to the ground. "Shit, shit, shit!" He looks all around to see his legs and chest tangled in the remnants of a low barbed-wire fence. He's in excruciating pain and bleeding in little places all over. "Are you kidding me?"

It takes forever to free himself from the wire, because each angry barb of the long rusty coiled wire has pierced a piece of fabric or a piece of his skin. The wire isn't just across his front, either; he is lying on top of some of it. The pain is fierce at first but only lasts a few seconds, and none of the little cuts are bad. Now a different pair of jeans bear the color of blood, this time his own. By the time he has finished extracting himself from the barbed wire, the child is no longer in sight.

"Well, I tried."

He checks the time on his phone and decides to waste a few minutes in the Scary Giant Corn Maze before showering again and changing for lunch. *Did I bring another pair of pants?* He has been looking forward to exploring some of the parts he hadn't seen the night before, but along the way, he finds himself wishing Julia was there to share it with him. And then his mood worsens, for as much as he likes being at the farm and enjoying the change of pace, it is making him sad to see all the children running along the pathways, dodging in and out of the dead ends and laughing with their families. He wants to play catch and visit a corn maze with kids of his own. The loneliness overwhelms him, and he resolves to bring up the subject with her again. Tonight. Maybe this time, he can convince her. When he arrives at the entrance to the maze, the taller burlap boy manning the ticket booth makes him wonder if Ma and Pa ever let the kids take off their masks. He pays for the admission and enters.

About ten minutes into his stroll, Josh discovers he is in another of one of those circles that are populated with pumpkin people, like a couple they'd seen the night before. A valet in a tailcoat is holding a tray with a champagne glass, and it catches his eye, because draped over his free arm is Tara's bright-red sweater. The last time he'd seen it, she was wearing it at breakfast.

He looks around the circle and strains to see through the thick corn wall, wishing he has x-ray vision. Then he reconsiders. In this case, he wouldn't want to see too much. "Tara! Are you decent? Hey, Tara, you two aren't the only ones out here in there—whatever, you know. Think of the children!" He chuckles. "Come out, come out, wherever you are. Ha-ha."

# 36

The corn stubble from the mower that cut the paths months ago is still sharp in some places, so it is difficult to walk on with bare feet, but at this point, Tara thinks any path is better than the mud. It turns out the path she is now on isn't actually that far from where she'd gotten stuck, but those thirty feet or so have been a long slog, and she treats herself to a few moments to catch her breath and rub her feet.

*Voices!* She hears a muffled conversation between a couple of men she can only see from the back, and they are just ahead on the left. Inspired by the possibility of getting help, it only takes her a couple of moments to join them. "Hey, guys, am I glad to see you! You wouldn't believe what I've been through. Can you help me, please?" She is happy to see one of the men is her old friend the clown again. "Lucas! Man, was I pissed at you back there! Will you please get me out of here?"

The clown doesn't speak.

"Lucas, please! You'll never believe what happened to me. I was trying to keep up with you, when I got stuck in the mud, and now I'm trying to get around on one shoe. If you could just . . ."

The clown isn't paying any attention to her. Instead, he is staring at a woman's body lying facedown on the ground at their feet. "Oh my god. So this is what the emergency was. Is she all right?" Again the clown does not answer, but from behind her come the two strong arms belonging to Leatherface, who wrestles her face down onto the stubbly ground, bruising and breaking the skin on her arms and face in numerous places.

"What the fuck! Hey, let go of me! Lucas, help me! What's going on? Lucas!"

Leatherface stands up, leaving her flat out on the ground. She is a little dazed and very confused, but she is horrified when she lifts her head and finds herself eye to eye with her friend Shelly. A few flies are dancing on the corners of her mouth, and rigor mortis has already set in. "Shelly, can you hear me? Are you all right?" Tara shakes Shelly's body gently. "Shelly, answer me!"

"She can't hear you, bitch!" growls the clown as he throws Shelly's petite body over Leatherface's massive shoulders. During that split second, when they are shifting Shelly's body around to balance her weight, Tara bolts up and sprints away from them. Her feet are bleeding as she charges down the straightaway, but she doesn't care. A quick look behind her shows the clown is closing in. They are both fast, but she is faster, and she intentionally slows down to let him catch up a little. When he is close enough, she flings the shoe she's been carrying at him, and the heel whacks him hard in his ugly face, causing him to stop dead in his tracks for a moment. *Good shot. Glad I had brothers who taught me how to throw.* Tara then picks up speed and races on ahead, leaving the clown far behind.

# 37

He has just about given up finding Tara, when Dillon comes running toward him. "Josh! Oh my god, Josh! I'm glad I found you. The kid at the entrance told me you were in here. We've got to get out of here. Turns out that Carrie woman was right, and now I can prove she's dead. Bad things have been—"

"Hey, slow down, pardner. Whaddya talkin about?"

"Seriously, Josh, Carrie really is dead. I found her hat, and it was all covered with blood, and Julia—"

"A bloody hat?" Josh interrupts, laughing a little. He deliberately is speaking slowly to counter Dillon's staccato delivery. "Do I have to explain props to you? Boom! Take that! Hardy har har."

"Josh, it's not funny. And Julia thinks she was raped. She was so out of it last night when you got in bed with her, she didn't even know it was you."

"Raped? Who? By me? I wasn't in her room last night. I was wasted. Did somebody screw my wife last night? Who the fuck did it, Lucas? Is he screwing all the women?"

"Wait! You weren't there? Ma says you were up walking around. She says she heard you two all night, bed squeaking and everything. Are you sure?"

"I think I'd know, don't you?"

"Well, why would Ma lie about that?"

"Who cares about what Ma said! What about my wife?"

"Well, hold on now, Josh. I said she *thinks* she was raped. Says it happened in her sleep, but we don't see how it could have, because she had locked her room."

Josh is furious. "Why the fuck didn't you tell me this right away?"

"Hey, asshole, I'm your friend, remember? Don't kill the messenger. Now you slow down and let me explain. OK, so after I left you earlier, I went back to the house. *You* asked me to check in on *your* wife, remember? You were pretty busy with your flask. Okay, so I was in the house, and I heard Julia screaming, *your wife* screaming. Ma and I raced to her room, and she was hysterical."

"Christ! I'm sorry, Dillon. So what do you mean she *thinks* she was raped?"

"Well, here's the thing. Look, she made me promise not to tell you this, but she's been on antidepressants. And last night, she took a few too many sleeping pills."

"What? She's seeing a shrink? She's popping pills? How did I not know this?"

"But wait. Then on top of all the pills and the booze, Ma gave her some homemade sleepy-time hot cocoa. I'm sure she wouldn't have given it to her had she known about the other stuff, but Ma and I think Julia was hallucinating a little, that's all."

"But, Dillon, a woman has to know if she was raped or not, unless . . . poor Julia."

"Yeah, she was pretty adamant about it, but I think she was probably still screwed up from the drugs."

"I hope that's all it was, but crap. No wonder we've been having problems. It all makes sense now about putting off having a family, the mood swings, always sleeping. Julia's got real stuff going on I didn't know about."

"Anyway, we're getting out of this place now. She's getting you both packed, and I said I'd bring you and Tara back. Where is she, by the way? Have you seen her?"

"Haven't seen her yet, but now I'm not sure I want to, because I found her sweater hanging on one of those scarecrows. Looks like she and Lucas didn't waste any time getting down to it."

The maze is filling up with visitors and becoming a little crowded. Since Josh and Dillon are just standing in the path, those wanting to go faster bustle on around them. Two or three kids are playing catch, and whatever they were throwing goes sailing over one boy's head and lands at Dillon's feet. *Kerplop!* The intended receiver doesn't even bother to look back; he's already lost interest, and he chases forward after his friend farther on into the maze. When he looks down at the muddy foreign object, Dillon sees the *Ferragamo* label staring back at him. He stoops to get a closer look, and after wiping away some of the mud, he recognizes it as one of the shoes that had kicked him under the table a couple times this morning. *There can't be too many other people silly enough to be wearing Ferragamos out here*, he thinks.

"What the hell? Tara must be hobbling around in there on one foot. I don't like the looks of this. And the sweater. She's not the type to chuck her designer stuff. Maybe it's worse than I thought? Maybe Lucas is in on this. Josh, you've got to find her right now and help her get out of there. We'll leave as soon as she can get her stuff together. Now I'm thinking about Carrie's bloody hat again. Sorry I can't help you find Tara, but I've got to get back to the house and help Julia get out."

"I think I should be the one to get my wife."

"Not a good idea. You guys are too volatile right now to get it together. I'll handle her. Besides, I know where she is. You focus on helping Tara."

"Dillon, Dillon. Okay. I'll find her as fast as I can, but don't get spun out of control again. I'm sure she's fine. Jesus, I mean, how far could she have gotten with only one shoe?"

\* \* \*

Pain is of no consequence now that Tara can see her way out. There are lots of people up ahead, and as soon as she gets close to them, she'll be safe. But she was looking backward while she was running forward, so she didn't see the small child extend his short leg out into the path. Tara trips and falls hard, and she screamed her lungs out loud and long.

# 38

At the sound of someone screaming bloody murder, everyone in the maze stops to listen. "What the hell? *Tara!*" Josh and Dillon hightail it in the direction of the scream. Getting in *that* direction, though, requires winding around a couple of crazy complicated circles and doubling back a few times, but soon they meet up with a growing crowd of concerned people who have already formed a circle around someone.

"Oh my god! It's Tara, I knew it!" Dillon's mind is speeding as he realizes that little by little, event by event, the day is unfolding just as Carrie had cautioned. They barrel their way through the crowd. "Move away! Move away, please! She's with us! Sorry! Excuse us!"

"What happened?" shouts Josh. As the wall of people parted to let them in, they see a scared little girl being comforted by a middle-aged woman. She has wrapped her frail young arms tightly around the woman's neck, and she is crying her eyes out.

"She said she saw a bug," two or three people offered at about the same time.

"Wow, that kid's got a set of lungs on her," says another.

Tara's simultaneous screaming had been no match for the terrified seven-year-old's.

"Are you her father?" asked the woman, relieved at seeing Josh.

They have been speed walking the ten or fifteen minutes it would take to get all the way back to the other side of the maze and out, when another burlap kid runs up to them. She tugs at Josh's shirt and says in a surprisingly normal voice, "Ma sez to tell you yer friend Mrs. Roberts turned up and that she and Miss Tara are in the corn maze."

"What? You kids can speak? OK, she finally showed up, Dillon. So see, Shelly is here and not dead, and actually now nobody's dead, and so nobody is a murderer after all."

"I can't take any more of this." Dillon just stands shaking his head.

"Okay, so let's review. Putting aside Julia's dream sequence for the moment, we've got Shelly and Tara in the maze somewhere, and we've established they aren't dead. And given that Shelly's alive, Ma wouldn't have had to kill Carrie now, would she? Unless, of course, she just felt like it—you know, for sport or something. So what do you think? Is Carrie still dead, or do you want to change your mind about her too?" Josh punctuates his sarcastic humor with a couple of friendly pokes to Dillon's arm.

"OK, you don't have to dig it in. I hate it when you play Perry Mason, and I can't believe I got swept up in all this. It was getting to be a little like *Ten Little Indians* around here."

"Anything else from you two supersleuths?"

"Oh yeah. Julia told Ma to call the police and a doctor. She did, and they're both on their way."

"Great!" he adds sarcastically. "Good thing Perry Mason is here after all. Hey, since the phone's working now, does this mean we have Internet?"

"But Josh, wait. That's the other thing. How could she have called the doctor if the phone line was dead?"

"Maybe she said she *would* call and forgot it was down, or maybe it got fixed. You are pretty hard on ol' Ma."

"No, Josh, she said they were on their way. And I remember her specifically saying the phone company couldn't make it out to fix it until Tuesday. See? If she lied to us about the phone, this means she could have been lying to us about a lot of other things. But why? It's just too weird. I'll go back and get Julia like I said before, and you round up Tara and Shelly. We'll all meet back at the house as soon as possible."

"Okay, but I'm dying of thirst, and since now none of this is as urgent as you thought, do we have time for me to buy you a drink?" Dillon nods, and after they exit the maze, they walk the thirty yards or so to the concession stand and guzzle down a couple of large lemonades.

"Are we good?" Josh asks.

"Us? Yeah, of course, but I'm going to feel better when we get out of here. Let's hope we can before the sheriff comes and complicates things."

Dillon takes off for the house, and Josh turns around to go back into the maze. He hopes the kid won't make him pay again. In the five or so minutes it took them to get their drinks though, they missed all the commotion. According to the buzz, apparently two guys, one wearing a Leatherface mask and one in a clown mask, had been hauling a woman out of the maze by her hands and feet. "She was yelling and screaming to call the police," someone said, "and kicking and thrashing."

"She was saying *they killed* her. *They're going to kill me!*" another one joked.

"I guess she was talking about the dead body Leatherface had draped over his shoulders. You wouldn't believe how realistic it was!"

"What will they do next around here?"

"Another fun day at Winter's Farm and Orchard!"

"Those two guys did a great job!"

# 39

**D**illon takes the steps two at a time and barges right into her room. "Jules, good news! I found Josh, and Shelly turned up! They'll both be here shortly, as soon as they . . ."

He is talking to an empty room. Almost empty. Lucy is sweeping over in a corner, and she smiles at him but says nothing. She has a ring full of keys on her wrist just like Ma's, only smaller. *If Lucy could only be more like her mother.* The lovely bed has been made up, and everything is pristine. There is no evidence, and he is furious.

"What are you doing?" he yells at Lucy, and she drops her broom.

"Beggin' yer pardon?" Lucy says, tilting her head.

"Why are you cleaning this room?"

"I always start with this room. An' after, I do room 12, an' room 11, an' then—"

He interrupts, "Yeah, I get it. But who told you to clean it now?"

"Ma, a course. Said Miss Julia wasn't feelin' well, and she wanted me to git it nice an' cleaned up extra special fer her."

"Good grief." He's panicking again. Not about Shelly getting murdered, of course, but now he wonders if Ma has been lying about Shelly being in the corn maze too. Did she send the kid with a phony message? Carrie said the kids were all in on it. *There are spies everywhere,* she'd said.

"Where's Mrs. Peale?"

"I dunno. Ma said she had to go."

"What the hell does that mean? Had to go where?"

"I think she had to go to her car or sumthin'. I dunno. Geez!"

As he looks around the room, he notices someone has already replaced the old broken lamp on the bedside table with a new old lamp. This one is brass. Next to it, precariously near the edge, lies a real live baby wrapped in a blanket. "Whose baby is this? The blanket is exactly like the one I bought Shelly for her boy. See? Saks Fifth Avenue."

"It's mine. A nice guest gave it to me, an' Ma said I could keep it," she says, adding a little curtsy for good measure.

"The blanket, or the baby?" He's angry and takes it out on her. He marches over and slides the child toward the center of the table away from the edge. "If he were mine, I'd take better care of him."

Lucy looks petulant.

"What the fuck? How old are you, Lucy?"

"Twenty-four and a half, going on twenty-five." Lucy lets out a *harrumph*. "Yer mean, an' I'm telling Ma." She scurries out past Dillon in a huff and slams the door behind her. Thirty seconds later, the sheepish girl returns with her head down to scoop up the poor baby she forgot to take.

"Fergit sumthin'?" he mocks.

Her exit from this room is far less grand than the one the night before with Julia.

Dillon turns and storms out of the room, calling into all the rooms he passes on his way down the hall. "Julia! Julia! Where are you? Answer me!" It is a quiet and empty house.

He hesitates at the door with the wreath before he tries the knob, but the door is locked. Time to review again. The baby in Lucy's custody is undoubtedly Shelly's, and he's sure the blanket was his gift, so Shelly must have gotten here at some point. And she may or may not be alive. The blood on Carrie's beret, which he saw with his own eyes and believed was real, might actually be real after all. So Carrie could still be dead. Ma could have lied about Tara being in the maze—or maybe not. Julia, who is not here, may or may not have been raped by someone who entered her locked room. And finally, Josh, who right now thinks everything is fine, might also be in danger. *Shit! Now what?*

Dillon runs down the hall to their original room. Nothing there. No suitcase, no clothes. They've all been packed up, so maybe nitwit Lucy was right. Maybe she did go to the car with the luggage, or maybe she left her luggage downstairs and she just left for a moment to bring the car around. On a whim, he goes back to Julia's room and finds the ring of keys Lucy set down when she picked up the baby. He grabs the ring and put it in his jeans pocket. *These keys might come in handy.* Then he locks the door to her room from the inside to buy a little time.

His heart is racing, and his head is spinning, but he is trying to prioritize his next moves. Julia is probably all right for the moment, so since he's alone in the house, maybe he can find the answer to the other thing that's been nagging at him. *How the hell did the rapist get into her room when the door was clearly locked?* If he can't find evidence of any other way into her room, he can rest easy about the rape. It can't have happened.

He scans the room, looking for a clue. It is a big room, but there can't be many possibilities, so he starts with the obvious. Kneeling at the side of the bed, he grabs the bed skirt, takes a breath, and then flips it up. Nothing below. *C'mon, Dillon, a trapdoor on the floor of a second-floor bedroom? Get real.* He looks around the room one more time. No air registers large enough to slip through. There are a couple of chairs, a little sofa, a table, the baby crib—that was all. There simply is nowhere else for anyone to hide in the room except for the closet. He walks over and opens the door. There are lots and lots of linens stacked on the shelves—that was all. It must be where they keep them all; there are so many. On the clothes rod hang a few mismatched coat hangers.

He is about to give up and close the door, when a spider skitters across the floor and catches his eye. It passes over a scrape in the wood finish of the floor in the shape of an arc. When he is sure it is gone, he kneels down on the floor and traces the scuff with his fingers—all the way to the edge of one of the shelves. He knows something substantial must swing out over it to have made that mark. He tugs at one of the shelves in front of him. Nothing. He tugs again a little harder, and a catch releases. The entire shelf unit swings open, revealing a dark passage with exposed beams and insulation.

*Holy crap!* It's narrow, but it's tall enough that he only has to stoop a little. With the dark passageway illuminated by his flashlight app, he sees more of those creepy dolls like the ones downstairs in Ma's nursery. They are scattered here and there on the floor and tucked into rips in the insulation. The bodies of a couple dolls have been separated from their heads. *Sadistic little kids must play in here.*

The floor creaks as he moved, and he is so paranoid that with each creak, he stops and looks back around to see if anyone is following him. Then another sound behind him. "Julia?" No response. "Jules?" he tries again, louder, beginning to feel cramped and claustrophobic. *I guess not.* He shines his phone's light into the void behind him. Nothing. He lingers there for a moment and then swings the light back around to illuminate the void in front. This time, he thinks he definitely hears something behind him, but instead of turning to check behind him, he scrambles forward as fast as he can. The passageway ends in a tee. He looks left, then right, then left again before going left, where after a few feet, he runs into a wall with a big number 9 scrawled on it in reflective white paint. Wall number 9 is really a secret door, and when he ran into it, he pushed it open too hard and too fast. The other side of the door is disguised as a decorative wall panel, and when it swings open, it bangs against a wall mirror in just the wrong spot. Dillon's entrance into the room is announced by a loud crash and the shattering of the full-length wall mirror into a thousand pieces.

"Crap! Seven more years!"

# 40

The room was in utter disarray. Mounds of clothes spill out from a couple open suitcases and polka-dot pajama bottoms are draped over the back of a chair. Old newspapers and clippings are strewn everywhere. *Where to start?*

He sits down on the edge of the unmade bed and scans an article circled with a marker in a brittle newspaper that is already opened flat: *Georgetown University Students Vanish. Last Seen Camping.* Faded photos of the missing attractive young men accompany the faded article. There is another article about persons missing in the area—and another. *More Appalachian Trail Hikers Missing.* They date back almost twenty years. *My god, Carrie actually did do her homework.* There's another small lined spiral notebook opened to a page with a diagram on it. Frantic arrows point from here to there and over there to over here, but all of them ultimately meet at one name: Ma Winters.

*Noises!* Someone is coming down the hallway outside the room. Now they are outside the door. He holds his breath, careful not to make a single sound. The person has gone past the door now and is down the hall. While he stands motionless, he looks around the room for something he can use to defend himself. Maybe the lamp. He doesn't want to make any noise by walking across the creaky floor, so he stretches over to grab it. But he stretches too far and loses his balance and knocks it off the bedside table instead of grabbing it. It shatters. Two things shatter. What are the odds? *It really wasn't that loud. Maybe they didn't hear it.*

Footsteps again. *Shit!* He uses a facecloth he finds stacked with the other fresh towels to pick up a long shard of the broken lamp for a weapon, and he tiptoes toward the door. Just as he reaches for the porcelain doorknob, someone taps on the door. "Hey! Anybody in there?"

It is Tara. He can exhale now. He casts away the shard and unlocks the door, and they stare at each other, speechless.

"God, Tara, what happened to you?"

"They tried to kill me, Dillon."

"Who? Why?"

"Lucas and that guy Leatherface from last night, they both were. They caught me and were hauling me out of the maze right through a crowd of people, and since everyone thought it was part of the act, nobody helped me, the ignorant fucks. But I managed to kick Lucas in the nuts, and they dropped me for a minute, and I got away."

"Lucas was trying to kill you? Why?"

"I found Shelly dead in the maze, and they saw me when I found her. So I guess they needed to get rid of me, so I wouldn't be able to tell anyone."

"Oh, no. Then Shelly *is* dead."

"Very dead. Leatherface had her body over his shoulders when they were carrying me out. Dillon, we've got to get out of here—*now*! They'll be coming for me."

"Shit. Now I wonder about Julia and Josh."

"Where are they?"

"Julia was in her room when I left to look for you and Josh, but now she's gone. And I just left Josh in the maze a few minutes ago to look for you . . . and Shelly."

"Wait, *you* were in the maze? How the hell didn't you hear me screaming?"

"Well, we did hear a scream, but it was—oh, never mind. We can talk about this later. Let's get out of here!"

"How? Through the front door?"

Dillon locks the room again. "Tara, there's a secret passage. I think all the rooms are connected."

"Whose room is this, by the way?" She picks up the polka-dot pajamas. "Duh, Carrie's room. What a mess. Surprise, surprise."

"Actually it is," Dillon clarifies. "Remember Ma told us this morning she had already left?"

"Well, she left in an awful hurry then. She didn't even pack her trademark clothing."

"Or didn't leave at all." He grabs her arm to lead her into the narrow passageway door, when her bloody foot kicks something that slides noisily across the hardwood floor until it knocks into the wall.

Tara bends over to pick it up. "Jesus, my poor feet have taken a real beating today." It's an iPhone. "Polka-dot case. I wonder what she has on it?"

"Tara," he protests. "You can't mess with that."

"It's mine now, and besides, she's long gone. Maybe there'll be something on it we can use against them when we get out of here. I want all of them to get the electric chair, and I think they still have that here."

It takes forever to boot up, but there is no password needed, so at least the phone is usable. And there, right on the opening screen, a draft video message is open—unable to send. *No signal.* She clicks on the attachment. It is Carrie's voice, but the video sputters. Her voice is a whisper. "My name's Carrie Masterson, and someone is trying to kill me." The recording cuts off. "Join the club." Tara's understandably bitter.

"What the hell?" Dillon is terrified and grabs the phone. The battery's dead. He pushes the power button, and it turns back on for a second before it dies again. "Okay, we've got to go." Now he's worried about his life.

"No," she demands. "I have to hear the rest."

"Okay, but we can charge it later."

They are rifling through suitcases and throwing open drawers, when Dillon remembers he has a charger in his car. "No, Dillon, this phone needs the old cable. It's got to be around here somewhere." There's a thud of footsteps on the stairs. Tara and Dillon do a double take. He points to the passageway. "Come on—*now*," he whispers with authority.

"Just give me another second, okay?" she says, desperate to locate Carrie's charger.

Tara knocks a pile of newspapers off the dresser. Then they hear footsteps in the hall. "Shh," Dillon commands.

Ma knocks on the door. "Yoo-hoo! Someone in there? Is anything wrong? I thought I heard noises or something." She pauses. "Hello, is someone in there?" Ma's voice has that same sweet concerned lilt it always has, but the jingle of Ma's keys sends chills up his spine. He grabs her elbow and jerks her toward the passageway, and that's where Tara spots the charger. It's plugged into an outlet right by the broken mirror. She grabs the charger as she disappears right behind Dillon, and somehow they manage to pull the secret door shut, milliseconds before Ma's key turns the lock and she enters the room.

"Well, I declare. Now I'm the one hearing things! Land sakes!" Ma says loud enough for the two to hear her from just behind the panel, where they are holding their breaths.

It seems like an eternity before they hear Ma back out of the room and lock it again, and the sound of her keys can't fade away quickly enough for them. They stood there stooped over in the dark only a moment or two before they inch their way away from room 9. Tara is in the lead now, and Dillon is not reassured because neither has the slightest idea which way to go.

# 41

She pushes open a door painted with number 1 this time, and they find themselves in what is clearly not a guest room. The twin bed along one wall has been carefully made, and the colorful patchwork quilt that has been turned down appears to have been made from discarded clothing. A couple throw pillows have been covered in tattersall and chambray. One wall is painted a dark red and covered floor to ceiling with gilt-framed photographs and pictures cut from magazines. What the subject matter lacks in curation is compensated by their esthetic arrangement within squares and rectangles of molding on the wall. The décor reminds Dillon of the *Downton Abbey*–inspired office on Capitol Hill that had been such a scandal.

In the center of the room sits an old Singer sewing machine with a manual foot treadle, surrounded by piles of clothing and fabric. The piles are all very organized—women's shirts here, men's and boy's pants there, accessories over there. "What's this, Ma's sewing room?" A quick look in the closet reveals jeans and flannel shirts, and on the dresser top are a couple of scary masks.

"This has to be Lucas's room. Oh my god, he must have been the one who raped Julia! Do you think he actually *did* kill Carrie?"

"Well he tried to kill *me*," adds Tara.

"Carrie was right, they're all in on it. I can't believe we let him take you to the Corn Maze! Fuck!"

While they're talking, she rushes over to plug the Carrie's charger into an outlet.

"Come on, we don't have time for that now. What if Ma finds us here?" She ignores him and tries to turn on the iPhone, but she is rushing the process.

"Look. I don't know what the hell is going on around here, but here's the plan. First of all, you and I are getting out of this house right now. We're going to take my car and drive straight to the police station. Then we'll come back for the others with the cops. If we run into Ma, we won't tell her what we're doing or where we're going. We'll just pretend everything's fine. Deal?"

They gather up the phone and the charger and walked out into the empty hallway. They tiptoe all the way down the hall to the door to Josh and Julia's room, where they can peek down the front stairway. It is clear. *Home free!* "Wait a minute!" Dillon has an idea. "Let's charge the phone in Josh's room. They won't think to look in here, and it'll be charged by the time we get back." Dillon quickly locates a working outlet and plugs it in, hiding the phone on the floor behind the bedspread.

It only takes seconds to run down the front flight of stairs, but it takes a lot more time to fiddle with the series of locks on the massive front door. When he finally figures it out, he flings it open and steps out to the front porch. Tara has been following so closely, when he stops dead in his tracks; she bumps into him from behind. An imposing Ma is standing two feet away.

"Well how's my patient getting along? Say, was Lucas in his room? Cause I wuz lookin' for him myself." Turning to Tara, she says, "What in the world happened to you?" Ma puts a hand to Tara's cheek.

"Oh, yeah, um, I was with him, but then we, um, got separated, and I fell down, and he said we'd catch up later, but then, um . . ." Tara's so rattled she sounds like a valley girl.

"So it's back out to the festival, then?"

"Yes, definitely. We're having so much fun. But you know, I think we may run into town for a minute to pick up a few things first." Dillon glares at Tara for giving away their plan.

"Town? Now that sounds like a nice idea. Y'all will enjoy that. But what about the sheriff, now? You wuz so all keen on havin' him come out right away, him an' Doc Starnes." She's looking right at Dillon.

"You know, it's probably not necessary. I think Julia took to heart what you said about her acting a little crazy. You know, the pills and all. She's actually feeling pretty good now."

Ma is unmoved by the information. "*Is* she now?"

"Yes, so I think we'll all be fine."

"So you'd like me to call the sheriff back an' call off the dogs then?"

"Yes, would you call him? Thank you. Oh, and do you know where my car is? I remember Pa put it somewhere. I think he had the keys too."

"Yes, y'all will have to check with him. He wasn't planning on havin' you move it so soon, so no tellin' how easy it will be to get at."

"OK, well, we better get going then, if we're going to get back in time for dinner." Dillon can't believe how well this is going.

"Yes, dinner tonight. I best let y'all be on yer way then. You's a long way's away from town. A long way's away." She steps aside and lets them pass. "But if you have to go, you have to go."

*  *  *

The parking lot is a grassy expanse with rows and rows of trucks and all makes and models of cars. Good thing his car isn't there, because they'd never have found it. Pa had said he parked the guests' cars *out back* so they wouldn't get in the way of all the day visitors.

"What do you think *out back* means?" Dillon asks, as they walk as fast as they can without looking like they were running away.

"I don't know, behind some barn maybe. Do you think we should leave Josh and Julia behind? I'm worried."

"Nah, I think they'll be fine. I mean Ma let us go without a fight, and she thinks we're coming back for dinner. Anyway, I don't think she's the one we have to worry about. I think Carrie had the wrong person. Lucas is the evil one."

They spend half an hour checking behind the buildings one by one and have no luck finding Dillon's car. Then they spot a larger barn up ahead on a little rise. It is a little far away, but it is worth the hike, because when they slide open the huge barn door, there amidst jacked-up pick-ups and beater sedans is Dillon's winter-gray metallic Prius. There is no sign of Josh's spaceship, though, but they can't worry about that now, because they have a more pressing problem. Dillon's car is locked. It is particularly frustrating for him, since he's become so used to it opening automatically whenever he reaches for the door handle.

"Why the hell didn't they leave the keys in the cars? I didn't see Pa when we came out here, did you? Wonder where we start to look?"

"Lookin' for this?" Pa emerges from another part of the barn, holding the key fob between his thumb and index finger.

"Oh, yeah. Thanks, Pa."

"Never seen a key like this'n before. Took me a while to figure out how to use it." Pa still reeked of booze and cigarettes.

"Yeah, they're a little tricky at first."

"So thinking of taking off now, are ya?"

"Off? Oh, no. Well, yeah, maybe into town. We were just going to pick up something for her, you know. She needs . . . well, we both need . . ."

"Yes, I forgot to bring a—well, actually, Ma has been so nice, we thought we'd pick her up a little gift. And Dillon has such good taste, he'll know what to get, you know, so we're going together. We wanted it to be a surprise."

"Well, ain't that nice. I'm sure she'll like whatever you git." Pa takes his time walking over to hand Dillon the key. "What in tarnation happened to you? Have an accident? You wuz such a purty gal before."

Dillon grabs for the door handle, and with the key in hand, it unlocks right away, but he hesitates a moment before getting in. "Thanks, Pa. We've had a good time, a really great time here. See you for dinner, and thanks for taking care of my car."

"Oh, and speakin' of yer car. Them tires look mighty low. Yep, they's mighty low. I must a run over sumthin' on the way to bring it over here. Farms, ya know, stuff buried all over the place, and ya never know what yer gonna run over. I'd be careful, if I wuz you. If ya want, I kin get Lucas an' one of the boys to fill 'em up fer ya."

Dillon sees his tires are almost flat, all of them. *What the fuck did Pa run over?* Ordinarily they wouldn't be drivable, but they're going to drive on them anyway, because the thought of Lucas coming near Tara again for any reason was unthinkable.

"No, no. You know, I'm worried if we take the time to fill them now, we'll be late for dinner, so I think we'll just take off now and get them filled up when we get to town. Thanks though." He gets into the driver's seat and starts the car. Aside from a few alerts and the headlights turning on, the car is silent.

Pa shrugs his shoulders. "Well looky there. Nice and quiet. I oughta git me one of those. Ma says my truck makes a ruckus." He waves them out. "Oh, here's a tip. If ya want to avoid all them cars leavin', take a right on this little lane here. It'll bring you back out to the road a secret way."

"Good to know." Dillon can't believe it is so easy. First Ma, then Pa. Next stop the police, and they'll be home free. *Either Pa has shit for brains, or maybe there really isn't a conspiracy after all and Lucas has been operating in secrecy.*

"Do you think we should leave a message for the others to let them know where we went?" Dillon begins to turn to drive back to the house and then stops. He can sense that Tara's on the verge of breaking down. "Oh hell, I suppose the old lady can tell them," he decides. He takes Pa's recommendation and turns down the little lane.

# 42

Josh dreads having to go back into the corn maze again. "Remember me? Hey, I think we're friends now, don't you think? What's your name, kid? I'm Josh." He offers his hand for a shake.

The boy holds up five fingers. Josh can't tell if he's doing it with a straight face or not, since he's still got his hood on.

"You're kidding, right? You want me to pay again?"

He closes his fingers into a fist and then opens them to hold five again.

"Look, this is like my third or fourth time going in. I'm just looking for my friends, OK? Can't you let me in one more time without paying? I'm a guest here, you know."

"Hey, can you pay or get out of the way? Some of us want to go in." Voices bellow from impatient people behind Josh in the line. Josh steps aside for a minute to let the others pay, and when they are inside and the kid has turned to look another away, Josh sneaks behind him and whips off the burlap sack mask by the top. A more grotesque head couldn't exist in his wildest imagination. None of the boy's features are standard, and their placements are all akimbo. His hair is patchy. "Holy shit! I'm sorry. I didn't know."

Burlap boy calmly replaces his hood and sits back down on the chair without making a sound. Josh is still shaking and is about to hand him another five, when he sees Lucas across the way.

"Hey, Lucas, buddy! I was looking for Tara so we could all go to lunch. I thought she was with you. And I also heard the good news that our friend Shelly was out here. Do you know where she is, by any chance?"

"I dunno. She wuz with me, but then sumbody told her yer wife left you this morning, and then yer friend Tara fell down and hurt herself bad, and yer other friend wuzn't feelin very good, or sumthin' like that. I get it all mixed up, but Tara knows all about it. Sound 'bout right?"

"Jesus, Lucas, I can barely understand you. Whaddya mean my wife's left me? And where the hell *is* Tara? I've been looking all over for her. I found some of her clothes on the ground in there."

Lucas shrugs a stupid shrug. "I dunno. House, I reckon."

# 43

The *lane* Pa advised them to take is just some packed-down grass a couple of other vehicles had driven on before. It winds all the way around the outside perimeter of the farm, and at first, they worry he'd given them the long way out. But soon enough, they can see that even going the extra distance with their low tires, they are moving faster than the cars in the endless line backed up at the regular exit. "God, we'd be sitting there for hours. Thanks, Pa Winter!"

After the first turn, it is a straight shot for a long stretch, and Dillon is extra careful to take it slowly, but with every rut, he can feel the rims of his wheel rims getting chewed up a little more. "We only need them to last until town. We'll hobble in on the rims if we have to. I don't care." *Small price to pay to get out of there alive.*

# 44

J osh takes off for the house and leaps up to the front door. It is
locked. "Why the hell is the door locked?" he shouts to no one in
particular. He is pissed and frantic. But then he thinks about it a little
more. On a day like today with the farm crawling with strangers, they
probably have to keep it locked. Still, he is in a hurry, and he pounds on
the door, "Hello! Hey, open up! Ma?"

No one answers. He knocks harder. Still no answer. He knocks harder
still.

"Hello! Hey, anybody home? I need to get in."

Nobody answers, but he can see a shadow pass behind the decorative
glass panels. "Is Tara there?" Josh shouts.

"No," Ma says without expression from behind the closed door.

"Are you sure?"

The door lock unlocks with the great click of an ancient lock forged
of iron, and Ma opens it just enough to look out. She is frowning, as if to
say, *Of course, yes, she is sure.* Josh elbows his way in past Ma. "You trying
to lock me out? Where's Tara?"

"We always keep the doors locked. Fer the safety of our guests. What's
the matter?"

"So where is Tara, and where's my wife?"

"She ain't here, Josh. *They* ain't here."

"Julia! Tara!" he shouts up the stairs.

Josh marches straight down the narrow main hallway through the
door marked "Private Area, Do Not Enter" and storms into the Winters'
living room. It is unremarkable except for the vintage RCA television set
where Ma probably watches NBC. Nobody there. He calls out for Tara
and Julia again. Still no response. He leaves the private area through
the kitchen, then the dining room, and bounds up the stairs. He throws

open their bedroom door, expecting to see something, but there is no one there. What he does see, though, is a light peeking through the door frame of the room's closet.

"Jules?" he says, growing more and more worried. "Are you in there?"

The light in the closet goes off, and he hustles over to yank the door open to find out what's going on. He can't see a thing inside, and as he gropes for a light switch, the lights come back on. Standing under the clothes rod with the light's pull chain in her hand is Lucy, wearing an expression like a child who has gotten caught with her hand in the cookie jar.

"Jesus Christ!" he screams, repulsed from finding Lucy intruding on his personal space again. "*You* again!" In disgust, he turns to leave and bumps into Ma, who has followed him into his room. "Damn it! What's wrong with you people?"

"You'll have to pardon my Sweetpea."

Josh cuts her off, "No, I do not have to pardon your Sweetpea! She never stops leaving me alone! Now where's my wife?"

"I wuz trying to tell you, Josh, but ya wouldn't let me finish. They all went to town. That purty Tara and yer friend Dillon. I think yer wife wanted to go with them too. You just missed 'em."

"What? That doesn't make sense. I was just in the corn maze with Dillon and—" He stops himself and realizes how awkward it would be to explain the situation any further. "Forget it." Josh feels resentment building. "So they left me all alone, huh?"

"They tol' *me* to tell you, since yer phones don't work so well an' all," Ma consoles him. "*They* tried, but no one could find ya or get a hold of ya."

Josh's anger begins to subside. "Right, didn't help that I was—" Josh sighs, interrupting himself. "God, I'm an idiot. Did they say when they'd be back?"

"Yes, dear. They said they'd all be back here by dinnertime. Come on now, young man, don't beat yourself up," Ma consoles him, rubbing his shoulder. "How's about we both have a glass of Ma's special cider? I just made a fresh batch." Josh didn't bother to say anything; he only nods and enjoys the momentary back rub. He is still pretty confused and somewhat depressed, but he allows Ma to lead him downstairs to the kitchen, where she directs him to a stool at the kitchen island. He is careful not to get the cut-up tomatoes all over his hands and arms, but he isn't paying attention and sat down on a large pool of sloppy tomato juice that has dripped onto the stool from the cutting board. "First fake blood, then a cow pie, then my blood, and now tomato juice! I'm batting a thousand."

"Oh, was that *you* stinkin' to high heaven? I didn't wanna say nuthin', but glory, you need to change that shirt. Lemme wash it quick!" While Ma pours them each a chipped jelly glass of her home brew, Josh takes off his shirt and hands it to her. Fortunately for him, the long-sleeved Land's End T-shirt he wore under it has remained relatively unscathed and is wearable.

"Think I'll keep my pants on, though, if you don't mind. I can change back into the ones I wore last night when I go back to my room."

"They're right back here. Remember I washed 'em fer ya today."

Ma smiles and tries to lighten the mood. "All our customers have mostly left now, and the festival is over fer another year, so I'm gonna celebrate a little with ya." Ma's pint jar glass still has parts of the Ridgefield Farm and Orchard's Triple Crown Preserves label glued on it, and she raises it toward Josh.

Josh holds his glass at the rim with only his fingers, like slumped-over defeated alcoholics drink their shots in the movies, and he lifts it toward her but doesn't clink her glass. "Thanks, by the way. You've been such a wonderful host—honestly the best host—and I was nasty to you just then. I apologize."

"Y'all've been under a lot of stress. We all have. Happens to the best of folks and the best of couples."

"Oh, so you picked up on the problems my wife and I have been having, huh?" Josh sounds unsurprised.

"I know a couple's tiff when I see one."

The strain of his relationship with Julia and the craziness of the day has worn him down more than he had realized, and he has become uncharacteristically vulnerable. "You know, it's been seven years since Jules and I got married, and while it's been fun, it's been way tougher than I thought. And it only seems to be getting harder. These days we're always fighting."

Ma refills his glass. "The quarrelin' won't never stop, dearie. It's how you handle it that changes. Me 'n' Pa still fight every now and again, mainly 'bout the young'uns. Jest you wait 'til you have a couple of yer own." Ma sits down and faces Josh, who is wearing a melancholy smile.

"We're actually fighting over kids right now. About having them. I've been ready to start a family for a long time now. The timing couldn't be better, but she's—"

Ma cuts him off. "Oh, she'll be ready before you know it."

"That's the problem. I don't know if she ever will be."

Ma leans toward Josh. "That's nonsense. That's why we're all here on God's great green earth, ain't it? Life's all about kin, both the kin that's here with you and the kin that's yet to come."

"It'd be great if my wife believed that," Josh wishes.

Ma sits up straight again. "Oh, she will, she will. I can see these things." Ma smiles and waves her hands comically in the air, like she's a fortune-teller or a witch using mumbo jumbo.

He appreciates her humor and laughs along with the gag. "I hope so." After downing another big gulp, he looks up with a slight pained expression. "I don't mean to be rude, but I think you might have brewed a bad batch here."

Ma only smiles. "Oh no, dearie. It's supposed to taste that way. It's gonna help you relax and forget your worries, trust me. I drink it when the cartridge in my knees acts up. Works every time."

Josh suppresses a laugh, and he's glad Tara and Dillon aren't here to go off on Ma's "cartridge."

"Try it again." Ma's smile and eyes grow wider in anticipation.

"Well, thanks, but I think I'll finish it my room, if you don't mind." Ever polite, he considers making a detour to pour the rest down a toilet. "Hey, about my room, did you find me another one yet?"

"I'm on it. We'll take care of it when yer done with yer nap," Ma says, still smiling. "I'll wake you when yer friends come back fer dinner."

Josh thanks her again for her hospitality and then excused himself. On the stairs, he looks into his glass. He has only drunk a little over half of the glass, and he is feeling a buzz already. *Nothing else to do while I wait for the others. Let's see what Ma's brew can do.* He downs what remains and heads up to his room.

# 45

The farther along they go, the bumpier the so-called lane becomes, and at the end of driving a long stretch, they can see the road ahead appears to make a sharp right. Fearing what they can't see and expecting the worst, they stop just before making the turn. "Are you thinking what I'm thinking?" Dillon is rattled, and he holds his breath while Tara jumps out of the car to engage in a little surveillance before they proceed any farther. She peeks around the corner and can see that past another long, empty stretch, it looks like the lane opens to the highway.

"Looks all clear to me! So far, so good," she affirms, careful not to slam her door when she shuts it. "We're closer to the highway than I thought." They both share a tentative smile before he makes the absurdly sharp turn. He accelerates and speeds along the long straight section ahead of him but has to slam on the brakes when one of the burlap boys riding a rusty girl's bike comes without warning from behind a tree or something and cuts right in front of his Prius.

"Damn! That was close!" Dillon's neck and head are smarting a bit from when he jerked back against the headrest. The boy on the bike then unexpectedly cuts a sharp right and disappears into a space between some scraggy bushes. Dillon takes a deep breath. His nerves are frayed, but he is encouraged to see the highway ahead, and his foot goes back to the gas.

*Bam! Bam, bam, bam!* Fists are pounding on the trunk. *Bam! Bam! Bam!* More fists pound on the doors. He fumbles to find the door lock button, but he is so nervous he hits every other button first. A sledgehammer smashes the side window and makes his effort irrelevant.

Another big *bam!* Something from behind slams hard into the back of the car, and the air bags he'd never needed before are deployed. Six or eight new kids stream out of a truck that has come out of nowhere, and they whip off their burlap hoods, revealing their hideous, malformed faces. They buzz about the hatchback in a swarm.

# 46

Josh is a bit loopy when he gets to his bedroom for his nap. He empties his pockets onto the bed, and when he plops himself down, his cell phone and some loose change bounce up and fall onto the floor. He reaches down and gropes under the bed until he finds it. But the phone he brings up isn't his. This one is an outdated iPhone in a plastic polka-dot case, with the USB cable still connected. *Weird. Whose phone is this? Wait, it's gotta belong to Polka Dots. What the hell is it doing in my room?*

He flips open the case and turns it on. It opens right to the video Tara and Dillon had tried to view before the phone died several hours ago. Now that it has been recharged, it starts to play when he hits the arrow. The jerky video starts out with dizzying footage of the ceiling and then feet until it stabilizes on Carrie's face. She is holding up a photo of a couple of twenty-something guys in hiking gear, and soon her narration begins. "Here's a photo of my cousins, Gary and Tom. They went missing hiking on the Appalachian Trail a couple years ago." Carrie chokes up a little. "Best I can tell, Tom ended up catching a cold, and they decided to stay in a B and B somewhere around here for a couple nights to recuperate. Then they just vanished." She pulls the phone closer, and her face fills the screen. "Since the police never could solve the case, I decided to try myself, and I must have gone through twenty years of local newspapers before I pieced together a pattern. It turned out their disappearance was only the most recent. Nearly every couple of years in the fall, somebody seems to disappear around here. It's usually a male in his twenties, and nobody ever has any information." She drops her phone arm back down again, and her portrait becomes smaller.

"After checking out as many of the B and Bs I could afford, I found this place. It fit their description, because one of the last things they told us was how they were looking forward to sampling the farm's famous apple cider." Carrie looks nervous. "I started asking questions about the Winters, but all the locals gave me the same answer: 'You'll love Ma an' Pa. The family's been around forever.'

"It only took two days for me to find what's been in front of everyone all along. It's the scarecrows. The Winters are behind all the disappearances, and they put it all on display for anyone to see. I found one scarecrow wearing Tom's Wisconsin State sweatshirt and another wearing Gary's hat from the Wisconsin Dells. I left them on the scarecrows for evidence, but I can show you exactly where to find them. As soon as I can get away, I'm going to go back to town to report everything to the sheriff.

"Something horrible is going on down in the basement too, I'd bet my life on it. The first night, I thought I heard people down there, but the Winters caught me snooping. I think it's where they take their victims before they kill them, and now I think they know I know. If you are watching this video, find a way down there. But don't do it alone!"

Josh just stares at her phone. "What the—" He is too groggy to process all this new information yet. He is sort of following her rambling, but he finds it so silly he loses his focus and begins to nod. He jerks his head up quickly when a motor revs up just outside his window. He thinks it sounds like Pa's tractor from the night before. How could he ever forget the loud knocking and smelly diesel? He struggles to stand up and remembers to stoop to look. Sure enough, there is Pa, rounding the corner atop the John Deere. He's about to go back to bed, when he sees it's dragging a gray Prius just like Dillon's. "Holy shit!" He knows the color well because when Dillon bought his car, he kept making the point to tell everyone it was *winter-gray metallic. Winter Gray, what a crappy coincidence.* He is a little woozy, but Josh needs to find out what happened and if anyone got hurt. His body lists a little to one side as he picks his way down the stairs, and he knocks a few photos off the wall on his way. At the bottom of the steps, he reaches to open the door, only to find he needs to deal with the front door's complicated lock first.

Once through the door, Josh almost falls off the front porch, but his determination fights the active ingredients in Ma's cider and makes him a little steadier. He nearly collides into Dillon's car when he circles the house, and from the back of it, he sees the banged-up rear bumper. The rest of the body seems pretty unharmed, until he notices the broken window on the passenger side. He looks for someone to give him an explanation. "Hello?" No response. "JULIA! DILLON!" Nobody answers. Even Pa is not on the tractor anymore. *Where the hell did everyone go?*

He is clueless about what to do next. He figures maybe they have been going around to the back, as he is coming around the house from the front. So he sprints all the way around the house and back to the front door in the other direction. Nothing. Nobody. Back on the porch, he decides to go back in. It is locked again. "What a fucking joke. I just went out!" He slammed his fists on the door, "OPEN THE DOOR!" He kicked at it. "OPEN THE GODDAMN DOOR!" No response. Finally, he slugs the door with his fist but regrets it two painful seconds later. He has regained some sobriety by now, and he decides to try a back door that he saw on his last pass around the house. It is locked too. *Safety fuckin' first.*

"Hey, open up!" he yells again. This time, he has nothing to lose, and he throws his whole body at the door. After a couple of body slams without success, he lands a strong well-placed kick, and the door jamb splits and it gave in. He shoves the door open and has to duck under broken pieces of hanging doorframe to get in.

# 47

Julia blinks a couple of times and wakes up. She's disoriented, and something smells terrible. The last thing she remembers is that she had been luxuriating in a fragrant bubble bath. Now she doesn't know where she is, except that it's dark and dingy and smelly. A lone sixty-watt bulb hangs halfheartedly from the center of an industrial-looking ceiling, and it offers inadequate and ugly light to the even uglier surroundings. The rough walls are thick and look like maybe they're covered with some kind of soundproofing or other kind of insulation. Across the room, two or three rickety metal cots jutting from the walls gives the whole place the look of an abandoned infirmary. All around on the floor there are random things spilling out of open crates and half-opened boxes, as though they've been ransacked over the years by people searching for things they had packed away but needed later. Bikes and hoses and forgotten sports equipment are hanging from nails on the walls.

To Julia it looks less like a storeroom, though, and more like a dungeon, because her hands and feet are bound to a cot just like the ones across from her, and someone has dressed her in one of those long, shapeless gowns insane asylum patients wear in horror movies. While the mattresses on the other beds are out of shape and filthy, oddly her sheets are spotless.

"Where am I? Help! Help! There's got to be some mistake!"

# 48

Finding no one in any part of the house that's above ground, Josh thinks maybe he'll take Carrie's advice and look to the basement for answers. The basement door in a house like this could be almost anywhere, but Josh opts to check the oldest part of the house first. He flings open several doors on both sides of the hall before he finds the right one. He grabs the doorknob and hopes his luck has changed and he'll find an unlocked door for a change.

He's lucky. Just inside the door is a small landing, and because the door opened to the inside, he has to go in and close the door behind him before he can turn around again to go down the steps. He enters and makes the awkward maneuver. When he shuts the door, the old latch made a loud, substantial *click* sound. Like most old basements, this one smells dank and a little damp. He gropes around for the light switch but doesn't find it immediately. The wall's surface has fallen off in chunks here and there over time, and his fingers need to explore all those changes in texture from the rough laths and loose plaster crumbs to the grime of God knows what from the past hundred and fifty years before he happens upon it. Where the switch plate should have been, though, his fingers find an open outlet box and a snarl of stiff old wires that had been bent and twisted many times before they were finally crammed in. The actual switch dangles by wires covered in grimy old fabric that passed for insulation years ago. *Jeez, Louise*! He yanks his hand back before he gets electrocuted. On the next approach, he hovers his hand above where he remembers the switch was hanging and then moves slowly so he'd be sure only to touch the switch and not the wires. It is one of those round knobs, and he twists it.

Nothing at first, but then a bright flash and then *pop*! It is Josh's bad luck the bulb filament's final hour had been reached during the previous visit. After a filament breaks, it's useless to keep turning, fiddling with the switch. Nothing will happen. But Josh keeps trying to turn it on and off anyway, because that's what they always do in the movies when switches don't work the first time.

After his stunned pupils settle down from the pop of the flash, he makes up his mind to go down the old-fashioned way. He forces his hand to inch along the Winters' basement stairway railing to guide him down the old wooden steps into the darkness. He slides one probing foot forward along the tread first, and when he can feel his heel nearing the edge, he lowers it until it finds the tread below. *This is stupid. I have a flashlight, for pete's sake.* He pulled out his iPhone again.

The sudden light disturbs someone or something below enough to cause a flurry of noises down and off to his right. Startled from what's happening on that side, he falls back against the left railing, which is much flimsier. Just as he feels it is about to snap off, he lurches back to grab the old railing again and regains his balance. His phone slips out of his hand and bounces down each of the remaining steps. At least the light stays on, and he can see where it lands.

Now it is his turn to be disturbed by the light, and he shivers, because it reveals the creepiest room he has ever seen. The ceiling is low, and the joists are made of rough hewn logs, some still hanging on to their bark. Ancient vents and ductwork emerge like tentacles from the giant octopus of a furnace that dominate this part of the old cellar. They snake around and disappear into walls and ceilings every which way, and all of it seems to be held together by haphazard electrical wiring and spider webs.

His phone has landed in a pile of junk. He checks the battery icon—3 percent. Crap! *I'm going to delete that game when we get back to DC for sure.* As soon as he picks it up, someone opens the door again, and the basement lights flicker on. While Josh can see better now, the picture is worse. Dozens of macabre scarecrows in tattered clothes with stitched and stained burlap sack heads lean together in odd groupings. Some look disemboweled; there is rotten and mildewed straw spilling out from their guts. They are splayed on the floor, leaning against the walls and hanging randomly from some of that old wiring in the ceiling. It is like the catacombs for pumpkin people.

"Holy hell." Suddenly the lights cut out again. He scrambles up the stairs to take his chances getting out of the house, but the door slams shut. The *click-clank* informs him it is locked again, but it also reveals someone knows he is down here. He puts his weight into the door, but it is secured now from the outside, and this time, he fails at bashing it open.

# 49

Julia hears someone from behind some of the boxes on the other side of the dungeon, and she stops her screaming.

"What the . . . ? Where am I?"

"Dillon? Is that you?"

"Julia? Where the hell are we? God, it stinks in here. Come over here and help me get untied, will you?"

"Thank God you're alive! You're tied up too? I just woke up. How long have you been here?

"I don't know. I just woke up too. Last thing I remember was in my car driving away to get help and something hit me from behind. Now I'm here, and I hurt all over. What the hell is going on?"

"I don't know. Carrie said something terrible was going on in the basement, and it looks like that's where we are, doesn't it? Where's Josh?"

"I don't know. Last I saw him, he was looking for Tara and Shelly."

"Shelly's here?

"That's what somebody told us, but I'm worried about her. I'm pretty sure Lucy has commandeered little Blaine. I saw her with a baby earlier today, and I just knew it couldn't be hers. The blanket was just like the one I gave her from Saks."

Silence. "Do you think they are going to kill us?" Julia stammers to get out her question.

More silence. "I don't know." He pauses. "Are you OK, Jules?"

"No, I'm terrified." She starts to cry.

"There has to be something wrong, some kind of mix-up. When Ma finds out, she'll fix things. Anyway, why would they want to kill us?"

"What if she's in on it?

"Ma? How could she be? She's definitely not the type. They can't all be in on something this weird. It doesn't make sense. Remember that couple in the news last year? In Germany or somewhere? The wife never knew her husband kept all those people in a secret room?"

"Dillon! You're not making me feel any better."

Quiet. "Jules, I hate to say this now, but I found a secret passageway that connects all the bedrooms. I think we've gotten into some serious shit."

"So someone besides Josh could have gotten in my room last night." Julia cries more now.

"Yeah, and it wasn't Josh. He told me it wasn't. But he and Tara and Shelly are all out there looking for us. We'll get rescued soon, I promise."

Julia can't speak; she's so freaked out because now she knows she has been legitimately raped.

"Let's both scream together and see if someone can hear us. Ready, one, two, three." They both scream at the tops of their lungs. And scream. And scream. After a couple minutes of yelling, the screaming peters out.

"Do you think anyone heard us?"

"I don't know. Hope so."

Silence.

Julia can hear him thrashing around on his squeaky cot, and she thinks maybe he's close to freeing himself. But then he stops moving. "No!" he wails. The next sound she hears is Dillon throwing up.

"Dillon, what's the matter?"

There's more moaning and gagging from behind the boxes, and he throws up again before he speaks. In the dim light, Dillon can see the stiff and cold body of his friend lying on the floor near his cot. Her bloody face is frozen in horror, and there is a large bloodstain spread over her midsection. "It's Shelly. She's right next to me here on the floor. And she's dead."

Without any planning this time, they both scream again and again as loud as they can. "Help! Help! Can anyone hear us?"

When she can't scream any longer, Julia cries.

"Shh. Wait! Stop for a second. Listen. Do you hear that?" There's a door off to one side of the room, and she thinks she hears some commotion behind it. "Yes! Somebody's out there. They heard us." They scream again louder than before.

# 50

"**H**ey!" he shouts at the door. Josh pounds at it, but it doesn't budge. "Open up, damn it." Louder sounds come from behind him down below, and this time he's scared. "Who's there?" He thinks he still has his flashlight app for a few more minutes, so he makes a quick scan of the area. The light is effective for illuminating things up close, but it's lousy beyond its depth of field and into the recesses of the cellar. But it's enough to see a figure scrambling behind the scarecrow corpses and along the wall. "Hey, you!" He's trying to sound tough, but his voice breaks, and he loses the figure in the darkness. "Answer me!"

He notices a darker space in the wall behind him, and in the light, he can see a crude crawl space about four feet off the ground. A soiled doll sits guard on the crawl space ledge, and fortunately for him, it's looking away. Josh takes a small step over toward a small alcove that's partially covered by a couple of scarecrows leaning together. He knocks them out of the way with his hand, and a hideous child pops up and glares at him before it scurries across the room on its hands and feet. It could have been Ticket Booth Boy or his twin, but who could tell?

Josh is so freaked out he trips over a pile of junk and lands on his back on the hard-packed dirt floor, and something tips over and lands on top of him. Josh and a pumpkin person in a cheap wig are face-to-face. He brushes it aside and rolls over onto his other side so he can stand up, but staring him in the eye now is a real live corpse.

"Holy shit!" He jumps up and hops around like a maniac, flailing his hands over his face and body to brush off any bit of anything that might have touched him. When he's through, he reaches down to pick up his phone. Like the person lying next to him, his iPhone is officially dead.

He hyperventilates and gags at the same time.

"Fuck, fuck!" He's horrified and scared stiff until from behind him in the shadows, the wide end of a coal shovel swings out to meet his skull, paralyzing him for real. Josh falls on top of the corpse, unconscious.

# 51

**A**t first it's a couple of fists banging then a boot that finally kicks open the crude plain wood door. It was stuck, so when it does swing open, it bangs against the thick wall. For that brief moment, bright sunlight is allowed to cascade down a set of steep ugly concrete steps until it illuminates the cement floor of their dungeon. Julia isn't able to appreciate the sun because her pupils have been dilated so long and she is temporarily blinded, but she can recognize the person who has entered. Without even looking, Ma reaches behind her and with one swipe flings the door to its closed and locked position as though she's done it a million times before.

"Ma! Thank God you're here! Dillon! It's Ma. She heard us!" Julia is ecstatic.

"Is that you, Ma? Hey, it's Dillon. I'm back here behind these boxes, and I can't see you, but I'm still glad to see you. Know what I mean? Ha-ha." Dillon is relying on his winning personality to get them out.

"My, my, I heard quite a ruckus. What's all the shouting fer?" She sounds a little petulant, but they don't notice.

"Somebody brought us down here and tied us up. I think maybe Pa or Lucas—I don't know. Did you even know this place was here? I'm glad you heard us yelling. Help Julia first, and then you can untie me."

Julia is thrilled to have Ma find them at last. "Ma, I'm dying of thirst, and my head is pounding. I could use a couple of aspirins. Do you have any?"

Ma shakes her head and walks right past Julia without stopping. In the corner closest to Julia and completely exposed sits an old ceramic toilet. Attached to the wall next to it is a small filthy white sink. Ma flips the toilet seat down and ceremoniously brushes off imaginary dust from the seat with her hand, which she then pretends to wipe off on her omnipresent apron. She turns around slowly and deliberately and sits down on her throne. From this regal vantage point, she can see and address both her subjects. But before she speaks, she takes some time to wiggle around to get her large frame comfortable on the old brown wooden toilet seat.

"Hmmm," she drags it out. "Do this, do that, bring me this, I need that. I declare."

Dead silence in the room, except for two unmistakable gulping sounds.

Then Dillon asks, "Ma? Everything's going to be OK, isn't it?"

There's no answer. Julia starts to sob again. "Is someone going to kill us?"

"Kill you? Kill you? Who said anything about killing anybody?" Ma was all smiles.

"Well, somebody killed our friend Shelly. She's lying over here on the floor next to me, and she's dead. No wonder you never saw her check in. Pa must have done it and brought her down here so no one could see."

"Oh, yes, Shelly. That was her name. Too bad about that one. Didn't plan on it. Almost got away this morning, but she just plain ran out of steam. A pretty little thing, wuzn't she?"

"Ran out of steam? What do you mean? Wait, you knew?"

Ma leaned forward in Dillon's direction and squinted to see Shelly. "Oh, there she is. Yes, I see her now. I swear the lighting in here is terrible."

Dillon was crying now. "What do you mean *got away*?"

"We were so surprised to get our baby back, especially Lucy. She'd been wantin' one fer I don't know how long. Thought it would be perfect, you know, ready-made, but now I'm not so sure. She dropped the rascal a little while ago running down the back stairs. Guess he'll be okay. It's a he, ain't it? That Lucy can be a real klutz sometimes. Don't know how many times I've had to tell her not to run down the steps when she's carrying a baby."

Now it's Julia's time to throw up.

"Look at the mess yer makin'. First, you ruin my doll collection and break my meemaw's lamp, and then there's that picture of ol' Uncle Gus you knocked off the wall." Ma pauses for the effect. "But that's probably not enough reason to kill you. Ha-ha."

"We'll pay you for all the damage we did. Just tell us what we owe, and we'll take care of everything, I promise. Just let us go."

"Well, ain't that nice. You know I think I'm gonna take y'all up on that." She pauses and looks around. "But we'll have plenty of time to settle up later."

"What do you mean, 'plenty of time'? Aren't you going to let us go? You must know there's been a mistake here."

"Let you go? Let you go?" Ma imitates. "Listen to y'all now."

"Dillon, I'm so scared!"

"What about Carrie? Did you kill her too?"

"Me? Glory no. But she wuz a nosey one, that Masterson woman. Curiosity killed that cat. That an' a chainsaw." Ma giggles a little. "Lucas an' Cletus might a gotten a little rambunctious with her."

"Rambunctious? You call that cutting off her head *rambunctious*?"

"Right in front of y'all too. But y'all is too stupid to know what ya saw. You and Josh sat down right in her blood and thought it was paint. Sakes alive."

"You're a freaking monster!"

Ma stormed over and slapped Julia across the face. "Watch your mouth, young lady. Show some respect for your elders! I declare, city gals can be short on manners!" She returns to her seat and makes a big point of smoothing her apron with her hands again, as if that would put to rest any previous unpleasantness.

"Julia, don't!"

"Where's Josh? Where's Tara? What have you done with them?" Julia doesn't care what she says now.

Ma turns upbeat. "Funny story. Your purty husband, he thought he wuz jest gonna do his thing all day long. Thought he had the run of the place. Ha! Cletus an' one of the kids kep' him busy and out of the way as long as they could."

Fearing her rescue squad might now be down to just Tara, Julia gulps. "And so where is he now?"

"Now? I'm not sure, but I reckon he'll be joinin' us soon. The girl too."

"You're all fucking scumbags!" Julia is spinning out of control.

She grabbed Julia by the throat. "You is upsetting me, dearie," Ma warns, tightening her choke hold. Julia screams again, and Ma throttles her harder. Then she pulls out a carving knife from her apron and holds it up to Julia's throat. "You better shut up right now, you pretty little bitch, or I'll cut you!"

Julia is reduced to whimpering. "Had enuf yet? I'm warning you!"

Julia tries to kick again, and Ma is about to continue her punishment, when a different door swings open.

It's Pa, carrying Josh over his shoulder. He's naked and out cold. Ma points to the cot next to Dillon, and Pa dumps him on the dirty mattress. She's frowning and walks over to take a closer look at Josh's head. "What didja go an' do that fer? I gave him my cider."

"Wuzn't workin' fast enough," Pa grunts back at her.

Ma snaps back at him, "Well, you ain't so fast neither. An' what happened to his clothes? Wuz he naked when ya found him?"

"A course not. I thought you said you wanted me to take 'em off fer ya. They's right here."

"We wuz gonna do all that later. Now cover his thing up with a towel, this is mixed company. An' don't fergit to tie him up good."

"Yes'm. You sure are bossy today, Ma. I'm pooped. I've had me a day!"

"Stop yer bellyaching and git on over here an' wake him up."

"What have you done to my husband?" Julia is frantic.

Pa pouts a little, but he bites the cork off the bottle of smelling salts he took down from a shelf over the sink and waves the open bottle under Josh's nose. While he waits for Josh to come to, he leers over at Julia. It only takes a few moments before Josh jerks awake and shakes his head. He looks up, and he's horrified to see his wife tied up on a cot and apoplectic to find he's stark naked and tied to another cot just like hers.

"What? What the hell? Julia, talk to me, where are we?"

"Josh! Are you all right? Did he hurt you?"

Pa turns to her again when he hears her voice. He's got a big wide grin, accessorized by a bit of spittle in one corner. He walks over to her, sticks out his tongue, and pretends to pant.

"Don't you touch me!"

"Why not? Don't cha remember me? Wanna have another roll?" The smell of gasoline confirms her worst fears, and she turns her head away in tears.

"It was *you*! You raped me!"

"What! You raped my wife?" Pa smacks Josh in the chest.

"Hey, now that's enough. Stop it, y'all." Ma needs to intervene. "I let you have a little fun with her last night, but now she's off limits."

Julia is hysterical. She and Josh strain against their ropes. "Aw, come on, Ma. Jest a quickie?"

"No! You already dern near spoilt everything by leavin' the cellar door unlocked last night."

"You touch my wife again, and I'll kill you!"

Ma walks back away from Julia and sat back down. "Now here y'all go, talkin' 'bout killin' again."

# 52

The door opens, blinding everyone in the room again, this time with the late-afternoon sun. Lucy waltzes in, looking ridiculous in an ill-fitting nightgown, no doubt belonging to a previous guest. Judging from the huge circles of rouge on her cheeks, she had apparently gotten into Ma's makeup. She drags her new baby by one of its arms, like a toddler carrying around a teddy bear.

"Sweetpea, look atcha now. All growed up 'n' all." Ma beams and looks around the room, expecting affirmation from her guests.

"You are all fucking nuts!" Josh yells.

Ma leaps to her feet, storms across the room, and slaps him in the face. "There'll be no swearin' in front of the children!" She returns to her throne and holds out her arms. On her way to sit on Ma's lap, Lucy gives Josh a little smirk.

He yanks at the ropes and looks all around him, desperate to find a means of escape. "What do you maniacs want from us?"

"Thought you'd never ask." Ma is all smiles again, and her delivery becomes more like a mother telling a story to a six-year-old. "Well, it's simple. Sweetpea here has taken a shine to you. We all have really, so Pa 'n' me decided we're gonna let you be part of the family."

Lucy bounces up and down on Ma's lap, braying like a donkey.

"What the *hell* does that mean?"

Nobody talks. Lucy looks down, and Ma looks left and right and up and around, like she's waiting for him to figure it out.

"What? What the fu—?"

Ma shakes her index finger at Josh. "What did I say about swearing?" She leans in close to Josh's face. "Yer purty ex-wife over there—she's already part of the family, what with carrying my grandson an' all. That Pa, he never shoots blanks."

Josh and Julia are stunned. They can't believe what they've heard. She gags and kicks violently at his cot. "You assholes!"

Ma gestured to Pa, who then punches Josh in the nose. "No! Not in the face, Pa! Sometimes I wonder about you."

A trickle of blood runs down and over his lips, but Josh tries to compose himself. "Please. OK, I don't think I got it right. What is it exactly you want me to do again?

"Let me 'splain it to you," says Pa. "See, when two . . ."

Ma interrupts. "We need you to plant your li'l seed in our Sweetpea here so she can have a purty child fer y'all an' another grandson fer me."

"What the . . . You are joking. Why me?"

Ma starts to lose her temper and begins to raise her voice. "Cause it's our mating season, stupid!"

"Mating season? You crazy people have a fucking mating season? Do you know how sick you are?"

Ma looks offended. "Now why would you go an' say that? We just want what you want. You tol' me today in my very own kitchen you wanted kids, an' here ya are. Lucy thinks yer real purty, an' she wants her own baby too. We all git what we want."

"You all are fuckin' lunatics!"

"Once more cuss word outta you, Josh, an' I might forget yer gonna be my son-in-law."

"Son-in-law! Over my dead body!" Josh thrashes and yanks on the ropes again, futilely. "Help, somebody get me the hell out of here!"

"Mating season's always been this weekend, boy. Every two years or so. Wuz for my ma, my meemaw, my meemaw's ma and my meemaw's meemaw. Date's wrote right here on the wall. That's when we is s'pposed to get the man part from outside the family."

When Pa lights a cigarette, Ma get perturbed. "Cain't you do that somewhere else?"

"Sorry," Pa says, crushing the lit part out with his fingers.

"An' take the girl upstairs with you. All this shouting is not good for the baby. No funny business with her neither!"

"It's gonna be my young'un too, don't fergit," Pa adds with a little edge to his voice.

With all her kicking and thrashing, Julia makes it harder to tie her up, but when he finally is through, Pa throws her over his shoulder and hauls her up the steps and into the outdoors. Retaliating in the only way she could, Julia vomits down his back.

"Where are you taking my wife?" Josh is desperate and beside himself.

Ma ignores him, but before Pa is completely out of earshot, she issues Pa another warning: "An' don't you go smokin' in front of the children!"

Ma turns toward Josh and smiles. "I think may we as well git started then."

Lucy is eager to get on with her big moment, and after she hops off Ma's lap, she turns to place Shelly's baby on the top of the toilet tank. Then she performs her version of a super-seductive walk across the room to Josh, who can't believe the nightmare he is living. Lucy is graceless as she climbs on the cot to straddle Josh, who is squeezing his eyes shut tight and shaking his head in defiance. On the next cot, Dillon's eyes are huge and teary, and he turns his head away from his friend and promises he wouldn't watch.

# 53

About an hour later, the door opens easily, and Lucas enters. He looks around the room, as if he were scoping out the guests at a party. Dillon estimates the time to be close to sundown, because hardly any light enters the room with Lucas.

"Why, here's my Honeybee!"

"I made you a cup of tea, Ma, jest the way you like it." Ma winks at him, and he hops up and sits on her lap, still holding possibly the only matched cup and saucer in the house. Now his body blocks her view, so she has to poke her head around one side to speak. "We ain't got all day, Josh. Time's a-tickin'. Seed needs a-plantin'." Lucas holds Ma's saucer, while she sips her tea.

"I can't do it, okay?" Josh turns away from Lucy in frustration. "No one can down here like this. You people are insane!"

"Oh, for heaven's sake! What's wrong with you boys these days? Back in the day a man sees a gal like Lucy . . . boom! It's done." Ma stands up abruptly, spilling Lucas to the floor. She locates her meat cleaver on the shelf above the little sink and raises it over Josh's head. Seconds later, she slams it onto the mattress with a practiced chop, only a few inches shy of his head. It all happens so fast Josh doesn't have time to flinch. The blade slices all the way through his mattress, not disturbing a single fiber on either side of the perfect slit, a stunning testament to both the sharpness of the blade and to her prodigious technique.

Josh is hysterical and tries to strike at Ma—tries but of course fails, as he is still tied up. "Fuck you! Just let us go!"

"Oh, dearie." Ma is disappointed again. "Now *you* is upsetting *me*." Ma puts the tip of her cleaver to the bottom of Josh's eye. "You best watch that mouth of yers, or I'll cut you up like the sumbitch you are. I only need one part of ya, and yer be surprises how easy it works when nuthin' else will. Man loses his eyes, can't see. Cut out the tongue, can't say much. Lose a few fingers,"—Ma pulls the cleaver back and wiggles all ten of her fat fingers in his face—"and a man don't feel much anymore. See where I'm goin'?" Now her expression gets icy. She picks up one of his hands. "One, two, three, four, five. Now you listen to me. Which one don't you need? Won't take me a second." She raises the cleaver up high.

"WAIT!" he yells now, trying to buy more time. Josh can speak, but nothing comes out. He just lies there trembling and staring at her. He doesn't know what to do. *They're completely insane, so there's no point in trying to be rational.* His instincts turn to survival mode. *I have to play along until I can find out what to do.*

She stares at him. "Hmm. I dunno, maybe we picked the wrong boy." Then she looks over at Dillon and turns back to Lucy. "Why don't you give the fancy boy a spin? He's just as purty."

"Okay." Lucy nods eagerly and climbs off Josh and onto Dillon's cot.

"What the hell do you think you're doing? If you think *I'm* gonna have sex with her, you're even crazier than I thought."

Lucy writhes around like she's being sexy, but Dillon responds by opening his mouth wide and sticking his finger in it, pretending to vomit. He tries to buck her off, and Ma is not amused. When she snaps her fingers, Lucy snaps her head to take further orders. But when Ma motions for her to get down, she pouts a little. Ma sits down on the cot beside Dillon and places her hand on his knee. "Dearie, we is simple folk. We don't want nuthin' more fer Lucy than what any man can give her." She moves her hand up to his groin. She squeezes hard, and he screams in pain. "Now can you be a dear and try again?"

"Stop it!" Josh is yelling at Ma now. "Leave him alone! I'll do what you want. I'll do whatever you want. I won't fight you. But I want to make a deal. What happens when I've done what you want me to do?"

"Now yer talking sense. After yer done with my Sweetpea, well, she's got five sisters—or maybe they's cuzins—just waitin' to get swoll' with child by you and yer friend over there."

"Five? Okay, so tonight and all day tomorrow. We can get that done, right Dillon? Then what happens when we're done?"

Ma was a woman of many faces, and the one she was wearing is frank and matter-of-fact. "Well, we have to make sure they all *take*, a course. And then since yer ex-wife is gonna be havin Pa's new baby, ya may want to stick around fer that happy day. Some of the other boys are hankering for young'uns, too. They all like yer other girlfriend that came with you, an' since I cain't get Honeybee innerested, Cletus is gonna go first."

"What about Julia? Are you going to keep her a prisoner too?"

Ma frowns, as if he's asking a silly question. "Don't you get it, dearie? It's *you two* we want. She's just a throw-in fer Pa an' the boys." Ma leans a little closer to Josh. "How many times do I have to say it? Y'all's family now. No woman is gonna wanna leave her new young'un now, is she? Winter's Farm and Orchard's gonna be y'all's home sweet home fer a long time."

Josh isn't comforted by what she says. "I saw the room with one of your victims. Don't tell me you're not monsters."

Ma smiles at Josh's misunderstanding, "Oh, dearie. They's the ones that didn't play along."

"You're making me sick," yells Dillon from off to the side.

"Oh, an' Lucy really wants a boy jus' like you 'n' Smarty Mouth over there, so it might take a couple tries to get it right."

"But you already have children! A whole freaking army! I saw them! They're crawling all over the farm." Dillon tries to reason with her.

Ma cracks a melancholy smile. "Oh them. They wuz practice for the girls. Pa an' the boys tried, but we couldn't never git a smart one out of the whole lot. Well, all the boys 'cept Lucas. I swear that boy would rather play with his scarecrows than—"

"Then do what normal people do. Have your kids get out and meet people! You don't fucking kidnap people and force them to mate with you!"

"We ain't interested in mixing with just anybody. Sometimes we get lucky like we did with y'all this weekend, an' like we did last year with yer friend Shelly Roberts."

"What's Shelly got to do with it?" Dillon is almost afraid to ask.

"Oh, didn't I tell you? Pa went an' knocked up Shelly too." She turns to speak to Josh a moment. "See, dearie, yer ex-wife's and Shelly's babies are gonna be kin—I think brothers."

"Stop calling Julia my ex-wife!"

"I remember her coming out last year like it wuz last week. It wuzn't matin' season, but it wuz s'pposed to be Lucas's *turn* anyway. But that Pa, he couldn't resist her purty face, so Honeybee traded his turn with him fer a new muffler or sumthin'. She wuz so out of it on our cider, she never know'd he paid her a visit that night. An' with the husband lying right next to her the whole time an' all. Glory! Sumthin' came up, and they got up an' left early. We didn't even know they wuz gone 'til they wuz gone. Stole Pa's baby, they did."

She walks over and picks up Shelly's baby, who by some miracle hadn't rolled off the top of the toilet tank, and she carried him back toward Josh. "It wuz a stroke of pure luck the good Lord had her bring Pa's baby back out here with her. Sweetpea here begged us to let her have it, an' Pa tol' her she could keep it, but she'd have to take care of it herself. An' I tol' her she had to take better care of him than she did with the last one, didn't I, Sweetpea?

"When Shelly found out, she put up quite a fuss, an' we had to move her to different accommodations, if you know what I mean. Tough cookie she was, yellin' and screamin' all the time. Julia heard her down here last night, even with the gag on. Then early this morning she got out an' thought she was goin' to get away agin. I don't know how she did it, but we weren't gonna let that happen, now were we?"

Ma lowers the one-year-old so Josh can see the face. "Didja ya think this beauty wuz Lucy's? Ha!" Then Ma takes a closer look before she puts on her stern face. "Lucille, did you fergit to feed him again? He don't look so good."

"I fed him *yesterday*!"

Ma gets contemplative and sweet. "An' I think you and Lucy'll make a real nice one. A boy maybe. No, a girl. Twins, maybe." She was so lost in her reverie she missed the mumbled conversation Dillon was having with Josh. "Okay, you two. Party's over. Lucy, git back over to Romeo there, and let's get back on track."

"Screw you!"

"Uh-oh. Here we go again. Yer disappointing yer Ma now, Josh." She smiles, and with the hand she's not using to hold the baby, she pretends to use her meat cleaver again. "Chop, chop, chop!" Josh spits in Ma's face.

"You pig!"

She smacks him across the face so hard his head bangs into the metal frame of the bed. "What the . . ." Josh's moans taper off to silence, his eyes flutter closed, and he's out cold.

"Dangnabbit. Now see what y'all went and made me do?"

Ma's exasperated, but as casually as if she were asking him to hand her a glass of water, she tells Lucas, "When he wakes up, maybe you can git him warmed up for Lucy, just like I showed you. You'll like that, won'tcha, Honeybee? Then I'm gonna chop off one of his fingers."

"Yes'm. All right." Lucas grins.

"Wait! Leave him alone." Dillon is shouting from his spot across the room. "I can do this."

Ma points and motions to Lucy, who starts up her sexy dance again.

"But look, if we're going to do this, I want to make it special for Lucy. She's all dressed up and pretty, after all. It's got to be romantic."

Lucy grins and continues to flail her arms in her awkward seduction ritual.

"I can see you're a good dancer, Lucy. Me too. We'd make a good couple. If I could only get on my feet, we could show everybody how sexy we are together."

"Ma, can we?"

"Sweetpea, I wuzn't born yesterday. That boy is trying to trick us."

Lucy pouts and stamps her feet.

"Oh, come on. You can still keep me tied on this long rope. It's not like I can go anywhere, now can I?" Dillon is gyrating for Lucy and licking his lips, like he saw Pa do earlier with Julia. "Besides, how we are we supposed to make the mad crazy love Lucy deserves like this?" He lifts up his hands, which are still bound by a rope.

"Ma, please!" Lucy pouts more.

"Lucas, whaddya think? Can you rig up the rope so he cain't get away?"

"Yes'm. A course." He takes out his pocket knife and walks over to Dillon. "Don't try nuthin' now. We is all watchin'." He cuts the rope from Dillon's wrists and returns to sit on Ma's lap.

Dillon is eager to finally be able to wipe the vomit off his face, chest, and stomach. Then he musses up his hair and stretches out his arms, takes a deep breath, and puts on a million-dollar smile. "Come to me, Doll Face!"

Lucy runs to his open arms, but instead of letting her hug him, he deftly positions her into proper dance form, putting her dirty right hand on his left shoulder and taking her chapped left hand in his right. He leads her at first in a slow dance to his own improvised version of "I'm in the mood for love," but soon their arms sweep up and down in an exaggerated seesaw motion, and the dance becomes more frenetic. Lucy is loving it.

"Now we're gettin' somewhere. Never thought he'd be the one." Ma is ecstatic.

He is dancing for his life, and Dillon slobbers all over her with big sloppy kisses, though somehow he is able to avoid her lips. She responds with her own goofy type of sexy moaning. The audience is mesmerized. Ma bounces Lucas up and down as though she has a child on her lap, and both of them laugh and clap at the wild spectacle. Dillon adds some mock pelvic thrusts to the wild orgy for good measure, and nobody even notices or cares that he still has his pants on, least of all Lucy. He twirls her around and around, faster and faster. "Ma, look at me!" She is the dancing queen!

One more spin, and Dillon is close enough to snatch up the meat cleaver Ma has left on the bed next to Josh. With one hand, he yanks her head back by her stringy hair, and he holds the blade at her throat with the other.

"All right, motherfuckers! *We're* getting out of here!"

Ma shoves Lucas off her lap and lunges at him. She has a knife now, and she is waving it at him.

"You come any closer, and Lucy's going to lose her ugly head."

"You don't have the balls."

With that, Dillon cuts enough of a little slit to draw blood.

"Mama!" Lucy cries out but not louder than Ma who is yelling, "Sweetpea!"

"Drop it, now!"

Ma drops her knife, and Lucas leaps to his feet and shoves her into Lucy and Dillon. They both lose their balance, and Dillon also loses the cleaver. Then Lucas swoops down to the floor and picks up the knife Ma has dropped. The tables have turned again.

"Well, well, well. Looks who's the big shot now? What was that name you called us agin? Oh, someone's going to pay now, an' we was bein' so good to you, spoilt you an' all. Sweetpea, yer little baby-makin' is gonna have to wait a spell while the boys here spend some time thinkin' about their future."

But Dillon can only think about the present. He yanks down a pair of old beige figure skates that were hanging on the wall on a nail and swings one of the blades at Lucas. The skate's toe pick makes a deep gash on one of his bare arms, and in the recoil from the pain, Lucas knocks Ma back onto the floor. He grabs Lucy's hair again and, in a surprise move, picks up the cleaver and hands it off to Josh, who had been awake and faking his concussion the entire time. During Ma's delusional soliloquy, he and Josh had concocted a quick plan to escape. With the cleaver, Josh quickly cuts through his ropes. Lucas regains control of his knife, and now he threatens the balance of power again. When Dillon twists the skate's toe pick into Lucy's shoulder, she screams, and everyone backs away again.

"You two, get in the corner over there! Now! Or I'll slice her head off with this rusty old ice skate." Lucas just snarls and Dillon twists the pick harder. She howls, and Lucas starts to go at him, but Ma yanks him back.

"Fuck you!" Ma blurts out. "Come back, Honeybee." He backs off reluctantly and joins her in the corner.

Josh had finished untying all his ropes, and now he's scurrying around to find and put on his clothes. "Good job, Dillon. You keep the blade on Lucy while I tie up these monsters." He secures their hands behind their backs and then tethers them to the filthy beds. "See how *you* like it, assholes!" Dillon yells at Josh to grab Lucas's knife and to hand him Ma's cleaver. They drag Lucy by her hair and tie her up too.

"Ha! Y'all is dumber than I thought!" Ma shouts up after them. "You's only puttin' off what's comin' to ya," she threatens.

They were almost out, but Dillon can't resist turning back to smack Lucas and Ma in the back of their heads with the blunt end of the cleaver. They fall limp onto their beds. "Fuck you!" When they yank open the door to their temporary prison, a tiny slip of silvery moonlight lights their triumphant march up the cement steps to freedom. It is evening.

# 54

J osh and Dillon run as fast as they can around to the front. Their
plan is to rescue Julia from the house of horrors and then find
Josh's car and get the hell out of there. As they circle around the house,
they hear laughing. Pa and Leatherface and a couple of the burlap boys
are leaning against an outbuilding smoking cigarettes. *So much for taking
Ma's orders seriously.*

"Well ha-ha, looky here, Ma must be losin' her touch!"

Josh raises the cleaver up. "Where's my car, you son of a bitch?"

Pa chuckles and wheezes a couple times before he starts a long
coughing jag. "Ooh. I'm so scared." From behind his back, Pa brings out
an ax that's a lot bigger and far more menacing than Dillon's cleaver. "Y'all
go down an' help Ma, boys. I'll take care of these sissies."

"Shit."

"Git back here!" They bolt for the orchard, and Pa sets out running
in hot pursuit. He turns on a flashlight that waves chaotic beams of light
around Josh and Dillon as he runs after them. The guys were hoping to
lose Pa in the rows of trees, but when they see how easily Pa's flashlight
beam can sweep across the rows, they decide the orchard maybe is not
the hardest but the easiest place for Pa to find them. They have no choice
but to duck down and hide as flat within the trees as they can.

Pa whistles an unnerving Appalachian tune as he brushes his ax
against the trunks of each apple tree. *Clank, clank.* The five-foot spacing
between the trees keeps the rhythm of the sound steady. The sound gets
louder as they watch the light get closer and closer. He is within a few
feet of them now, and they need to hold their breaths to avoid detection.
Pa stops short and drops his flashlight to the ground, and its powerful
beam is reduced to illuminating a clump of grass. He slams the ax into the

thick branches just above them, and dozens of apples pellet the guys. As he swings it back to take another swipe, Pa is surprised when Josh gives a powerful sidekick to his knee. The ax flies out of his hand, and the kick disables him long enough for Dillon and Josh to roll under the lowest wire of the trellis to safety on the other side. Pa is too big to follow them, and now that he will need to run the entire length of the row before he can get out of the orchard, they guys end up with a slight advantage.

They sprint out of the orchard at top speed, past the corn fields to where the woods begin and where Josh thinks they can probably rest safely while they figure out their next steps. Once they get to the woods, though, another flashlight beam sweeps and bounces in that direction, as Pa followed them to the woods. They duck the light, which passes over them, and they are about to consider doubling back, when several other flashlight beams crisscross in the dark from behind. They fall on the ground and try to be as flat as they can.

The beams scan the woods, first one way and then back again, but soon they fade and point in another direction as Pa and his posse left to search elsewhere.

"Josh, we have to be smart here. Look, we're outnumbered, and we obviously don't know the farm like they do. Your car is going to be useless because they probably have someone at the main road blocking the driveway. Besides, we don't know where they've got it, or the keys for that matter. We need to find a way to get out on foot."

"Once we get Julia and Tara, that is," adds Josh.

"And how are we going to do that?"

"Look, remember Pa said the best view of the farm is on top of the wind machine. I'm thinking maybe if I climb to the top, I can get the lay of the land, you know, and figure out the shortest way for us to get to the road."

"You can't do that. You'll be exposing yourself! What happens if they see you while you're up there?" Dillon tries to stay quiet.

"It's dark. I should be able to climb up without being seen. Besides, they'd never think to look for one of us up there. You go round up Julia from the house because you know that place better. Are you OK with that?"

"Actually that'll work fine. I can get in anywhere now because I still have Lucy's keys. I stole them from her earlier today."

"Where do you want to meet?"

"We can decide that after you find the direction we're going to go. I'm going with you to make sure you get up the tower and the coast is clear. It's an easy run from the wind machine to the house, and I can make it in no time."

To avoid detection on their way to the wind machine, they crouch behind bushes and pause behind trees and buildings, checking to be sure the coast is clear each time they change their positions. When they finally arrive at the wind machine, Josh creaks open the gate to the wooden enclosure, and Dillon hands him the knife. "Let's switch. It'll be easier for you to climb with a knife than carrying this damn meat cleaver all the way up."

Josh nods, and they make the trade. "If anyone comes, I want you to run. Don't give me a second thought—just run. I'll take care of myself."

"I'm not leaving you." Dillon starts to protest then realizes that he is wasting time, and they enter the enclosure and close the gate behind them. It is dark. Standing now at its base with the intention of climbing up, the tower now seems much taller than Josh recalls. Interrupting his second thoughts, someone suddenly stands up in the darkness of the far corner. Neither Josh nor Dillon has ever been in a fight before, but they both grip their weapons tightly and prepare for battle.

"Dillon! Josh!" Tara is thrilled to see her friends.

"Oh my god, Tara, are we glad to see you. We thought you might be dead. What happened? Pa and his goons are looking for you everywhere, and now they're looking for us too. You don't want to know what they want from you."

"It's a long story, but basically I've been hiding out right here in the corner behind this engine since I ran from the car this afternoon. Dillon, I saw what happened to you after I left, but I couldn't do anything about it. I've been peeking through the fence hoping to see one of you pass by, but no such luck. I was beginning to run out of ideas."

"Okay, well, right now, Josh is going to climb up the tower, and while he's doing that, I'll fill you in on the plan." Tara and Dillon lean on each other as Josh buckles on one of the belts and starts his climb. It takes him a while to get the hang of hooking and unhooking the strap every couple of rungs, but after climbing about ten feet, he's pretty comfortable with the system. He's less comfortable with the height. The ladder running up the side is not like any ladder Josh has climbed before. It's only about six inches away from the fat cylindrical tower that houses the drive shaft, so he can only fit his toes on the narrow rungs, not his whole foot. Now he's not sure his arms are going to be strong enough to continue climbing. He starts to freak out.

"I just can't do it, guys, I'm sorry." He speaks to Dillon in a half-whisper, and he climbs back down.

Dillon already has one of the belts on by the time Josh wobbles down from the final ladder rung. "It's all right, Josh. Here, take my keys and go get Julia. We'll meet at the corn maze because we all know where it is. You guys hide in the corn just inside the entrance. Go! And good luck!" He is taller than Josh and more athletic. The coordination of climbing and hooking the strap comes easily to him, and before too long, he is at the top. Pa had been right; from the top, you can see miles and miles in every direction, and tonight, there is enough moonlight to see even farther. After a few seconds of scanning the horizon, he points for Tara's benefit. "That way. There's a road just over there—northwest, I think."

Out of nowhere, the high beams of Pa's rusty orange pickup truck flood the scene, and the rumble of its engine announces the arrival of trouble.

"Oh, shit!" Dillon knows he is trapped.

Pa takes his time getting out of the driver's seat and saunters over to the edge of the enclosure. He lets the beam of his flashlight travel up the ladder rung by rung before it slides to a halt at Dillon. "Bingo."

When Dillon sees who else is down there and what else is about to happen, he screams, "Tara. Watch out!" She is looking up at him when a hatchet came flying toward her head, but she ducks just in time, and it cracks open a slat of the wood fence enclosure instead of her skull. She does a double take when Ma emerges out of nowhere.

Dillon is incapable of helping her from his position at the top, and all he can think to say is shout, "Run, Tara, run!" Now it is Tara's turn, and she holds up the heavy cleaver and swings it at Ma, who is surprisingly light on her feet. Ma jumps back and plays a good defense.

"Git the boy, Pa! I got this bitch!"

Pa starts to climb the wind machine ladder toward Dillon, who is still shouting for help. Up he goes, hooking and unhooking the strap with the dexterity of a man who has done it many times before. Down below, Ma is playing defense with Tara, intentionally moving the action back into the enclosure until she is close enough to reach a red button on the control panel mounted on the side of the engine housing. It roars to a start when she pushes it, and its roar can be heard for miles.

When he thinks he is close enough, Pa takes a swing at Dillon's feet in the dark with a hatchet from his tool belt. Dillon jumps up and hangs onto the nose of the propeller with both hands so he can swing his legs and avoid getting whacked. But he doesn't know how long he can hang there. He is afraid his hands will slide off the greasy fitting, and he is scared to death. *Clank. Clank.* The hatchet hits the ladder, and the sound resonates all the way up and down the hollow tower. *It missed again.* The third time, Pa swings it a little too hard and at the wrong angle, and it recoils hard from the vibration of knocking into the metal, and it jumps out of his hands, bouncing and clanking against the metal rungs on its way down to the ground.

Dillon takes advantage of the distraction and drops from the propeller to the top rung, where he can give Pa a hard boot to the face. Pa winces and scowls, but thanks to his ingenious strap and hook system, he avoids another one by rappelling around the ladder to the other side.

Tara is keeping Ma at bay with the wide swipes she makes with the cleaver, but she can't resist looking up to how Dillon is doing, and the clanking of the hatchet falling to the ground catches her focus. Ma catches her by the forearm. Tara slips her leg around and under Ma's and manages to throw her down on her back like a lady wrestler, but the momentum works against her, and she starts to fall forward, toward her opponent. But she's no match for heavyweight Ma, who tucks her knees and then, with both feet, gives Tara a huge angry push up and backward into the air. She sails about seven or eight feet and lands against a part of the machine, and the cleaver flies out of her hand and over the fence, leaving her unarmed and pissed.

The rubber grip at its end prevents the long metal rod she falls into from piercing her back, but the sudden and intense pain makes her lose her grip. To relieve the pain in her back, Tara gropes behind her to push down and away the rod that is poking her. *Ah, better.* But the relief is short-lived when she discovers the rod is the lever that has just engaged the propeller blades. They start to spin slowly.

The knife he brought is razor sharp, and Dillon manages to swing and slash Pa's left arm with it. Pa is strong though to withstand the pain, and he repositions himself to hang on to the top rung with his good arm. He reaches to grab Dillon's throat with his weaker wounded arm, but the rotating blades are starting to make him dizzy, and he needs to turn away for a moment to recover. Soon the blades will be spinning as fast as an airplane propeller, and the whole mechanism will begin to rotate three hundred and sixty degrees around its base like a floor fan, just like Pa said. The top of Dillon's head is only inches from the bottom of the whirling blades, and he is afraid the vacuum will first suck in his hair and then his whole head. Hanging on with one arm, he unbuckles his strap. While Pa is recovering, Dillon uses his hook to connect Pa's tool belt to a ladder rung. In a few moments, when Pa regains his bearings, he is able to reach down and unclip a hammer from his tool belt. He waves it menacingly up at Dillon. "I cain't wait to watch you die, boy!"

"You first, motherfucker," Dillon shouts back over the roaring sound of the blades that now are whirling at top speed. With one of his feet, Dillon crushes the fingers of Pa's holding-on hand, and the old man loses his grip. His whole body swings and bangs against the side of the tower, and he is hanging from his strap hook. Soon the propeller will be slicing through the side they are on, and to get to the safe side and down, Dillon quickly has to climb around Pa. When he sees the propeller coming at him, Pa decides to take his chances and jump. But when he unhooks his strap belt and leaps into the air, he doesn't realize he is still attached by Dillon's hook, and he is left dangling to face the oncoming blades.

Ma knows she is helpless to do anything to save him. It is too late to disengage the drive chain. Pa is going to be sliced to bits, and she can't look. "LONNIE! NO!" she wails. In seconds, the propeller shreds Pa's body to bits and scatters his bones and flesh and blood hundreds of feet in every direction, like the work of an angry industrial food processor.

Dillon has been climbing down two rungs at a time and is near the bottom, when the shower of Pa's carnage makes them too slippery to hold. He loses his grip and lands on Ma's shoulders, and they both topple to the ground. Ma jumps up and yanks her ax from the wall. She is boiling over with rage, and Dillon is now at her mercy. "YOU KILLED MY BROTHER!" She raises her ax and charges at him, when something slices through the air. *Whack!* Ma screeches, her hatchet flies into the air, and she falls to the ground. Tara leans the long two-by-four back against the fence where she found it and collapses on the ground next to Dillon. Their ordeal is over.

Lucy's keys come in handy when Josh needs to unlock the door to Julia's room. All the players in their nightmare had either been outside or in the cellar when he sneaked back into the house and up the stairs for the last time. Even though Julia is back in her luxurious suite, she is still tied to her bed. Without saying a word, Josh unties her ropes and ushers her out the door. This time, it is easy to slip out the front door into the darkness of the farm and to their meeting place in the maze.

It only takes a few minutes for Dillon and Tara to join them. "Tara!" Julia was ecstatic. "Josh hasn't had time to tell me anything. Are you okay? What a nightmare." All four hug each other briefly before Dillon takes charge.

"All right, we have to go that way, northwest. I saw cars on the road up there, and I'm pretty sure if we can make it there, we can get help."

"I can't believe we have to go through this freaking corn maze again. Are you sure it's the only way?" Tara is understandably reluctant to go back in.

"It'll be the last time, I promise," Josh affirms.

They dash through the paths, zigzagging at Dillon's direction. To stay on his course, though, they have to leave the cut paths and charge directly through the corn. It is dark and the corn is tall, and after a while, they begin to lose their points of reference and their confidence. Suddenly one of them bursts out of the corn onto an actual path.

Tara looks around. "It's that way. I recognize the path," she says, offering some encouragement.

"Are you sure? I thought this was the one that takes you back to the beginning."

"Oh, wait, you might be right. I don't know anymore. It's so different out here in the dark."

"No, you're right. The right way to go is the next one."

"Good. Let's go!"

They speed off again as fast as they can and make it to one of the straightaways, where they will be able to gain some ground and make some time. Julia is in the lead, and Tara finally feels they are going to make it. "Go. Go. Go! I think I see the edge of the cornfield," she coaches.

They pick up the pace. One hundred yards out. Fifty. Now only twenty-five. Almost there. *"Ouch!"*

A pitchfork shoots out from the wall of corn and skewers Julia's leg. When she tumbles to the ground, Dillon, Josh, and Tara can't stop in time, and they all three trip over her and crash to the ground on top of her. Lucas steps out and stands guard over them for the few seconds it takes Ma to catch up to them from behind. She yanks the pitchfork out of Julia's leg and dangles it over her chest.

"I've had just about all I can take from you, grandson or no grandson. Time to die, dearie!"

She is just about to plunge it into her chest when Tara flings an ear of corn and hits Ma dead center in the face. It only stings a bit, but it is just enough of a distraction for Dillon to wrestle the pitchfork out of her hands. But Lucas grabs him from behind by the neck and hurls him into the wall of cornstalks. The pitchfork goes flying, and he lunges into the corn after Dillon.

Tara scrambles over to snatch the free pitchfork before Ma can, and she jabs the tines at her like a lion tamer. "You stand back, bitch!"

Ma holds up her hands and does as she was told.

Tara can hear Lucas choking Dillon behind the smashed and broken cornstalks they both have just bashed through. "Dillon?"

His limp and beaten body comes flying out of the corn and lands in a heap. Lucas staggers out after him.

"You fucking son of a bitch!" Tara runs at Lucas with the pitchfork, but at the last minute, Ma steps in front of him. Two of the three tines of her meemaw's pitchfork poke all the way through Ma's midsection and out her back. She gasps and, grabbing her stomach, falls to the ground.

"Ma!" Lucas dashes over and kneels at her side, blubbering.

Tara picks up the cleaver and raises it over his neck, but he pays no attention. He is too distraught to care.

"Lucas, look at me! I can't believe you were part of all this. Tell me you weren't involved."

Turning his tear-filled eyes up toward Tara, Lucas whimpers, "But we only do it once a year, you know, to keep the family going." He is just a poor, stupid bastard, and she feels sorry for him. Without lowering the cleaver she starts to stroke his hair compassionately, knowing she is somehow going to have to finish him off in order to save them all. Across from her, Josh is so terrified his scream can't make it out of his mouth. Instead, he waves at her frantically with both hands, but Tara doesn't notice him in time. Executed with the swift precision of a Samurai, it takes less than a second for the full tang 17" stainless steel machete to do its job, and without its head, Tara's stunning torso and runner's legs teeter and collapse to the ground. Lucy stands triumphant behind her, one hand holding the Clown mask and the other Pa's machete, and she's coated head to toe in blood. It is not the blood, though, but satisfaction that adds color to her still otherwise unremarkable face.

# 55

*Ring, ring!* While she's the only one that ever calls, he still gets a kick out of the way his little iPhone sounds like the big old black dial phone back in the living room when it rings. He's begun to hate the intrusion, though, because he always has to quit whatever he's doing to answer it. His fingers aren't thick like Ma's and Pa's, and usually they dance gracefully over the screen, but this time, he accidentally hits the speakerphone icon.

"Whaddya doin' down there, Honeybee?" Lately, it isn't just that she checks up on him so often that irritates him, it's that she's calling him Honeybee. Lucas feels he's outgrown that name, and he hopes the guys didn't hear.

Sarcastic laughter tells him they heard. "Oh, nuthin'."

"Well, you better git on up and over here. Our new guests will be arriving any minute now."

"OK, I'll be along. I gotta finish sumthin'."

"An' tell Josh 'n' Dillon I'm sending Lulu and Lucy Jean down. They still ain't pregnant, and they need to try again. Tell 'em if they cain't do it, we're gonna git someone who can."

"Okay."

By their groans, he can tell Josh and Dillon have also heard that Lucy's twenty-three-year-old nitwit twin sisters or cousins—or whatever they are—would require their services again.

"He-he." Lucas laughs at them having to perform again. Then he taps Resume and picks up where he left off on his umpteenth game of Pumpkin Menace.

Ten minutes later, a telegraph sound announces another text.

"R U playin PM agin? Cumpny is here!"

When it was introduced during Fashion Week in Paris that year, the stunning Tiffany necklace hadn't been shown over a cheap blouse with the placket buttoned wrong on an overweight model with stringy hair. Today, though, it is only Lucy's second best accessory. Her first is the handsome one-year-old who is exploring the front porch floor beside her on all fours. The faster she rocks, the more the child is intrigued by the movement, and his grimy fingers are wandering dangerously close to his mother's rocker.

Across the lawn, Lucas's face and immaculate fingers are glued to his phone as he shuffles over to the front porch to assume his position next to Lucy. On the way, he stops to take another selfie with his newest pumpkin couple. The female dazzles in a sporty, if not slightly dirty, pair of Ferragamo midheel pumps, and the male exudes confidence and style with a Rolex Oyster Perpetual.

Dust from the car navigating the potholes announces the arrival of the new guests to the farm, but before they reach the house, Lucy has time to give Lucas a quick once-over. "Left it unzipped again," she points out.

Lucas zips himself up as the car pulls in to a halt in front of them.

The young guests pop their trunk and start to unload their luggage; as Lucy and Lucas walk over to greet them, she says, "Welcome to Winter's Farm an' Orchard. I'm Ma."

"An' I'm Pa."

Lucy tickles her baby, who giggles. "And this 'un is Joshua Dillon. We're the Winters."

"Howdy," the young man says, smiling at all three. Lucy holds her baby in her left arm and offers to shake hands with her right.

"Nice to meet you," his wife answers. "We're the Tolers."

"What do ya think, Pa? Ain't they jus' about the purtiest guests we ever had?"

"What a beautiful farm you have. I think we're going to be very happy here." The handsome young guests share a wink and a smile, because after all the bed and breakfasts they had considered, by some stroke of luck, they ended up picking Winter's Farm and Orchard.


The End

CPSIA information can be obtained at www.ICGtesting.com
Printed in the USA
LVOW11s0118271115

464317LV00002B/326/P